Frank Donato

Copyright © 2016 Frank Donato

ISBN: 0692712038
ISBN-13: 978-0692712030

For everyone who read this
while it was still a baby,

thanks.

You know who you are.

I Would
want to die
if I were
as old as
you

1

I STILL REMEMBER the bathroom stalls on planet Earth. They were honest.

I remember, too, that humans like me had a hard time being honest. I now thank God for bathroom stalls. Of all the libraries in the world, they had the best poetry.

***

My name is Hopeman.

I have been dead for two-thousand years.

There are quite a lot of us up here, waiting for the next planet to show up. God says our souls are going to be stuffed inside new bodies as soon as He finds a place for us to live. Supposedly, He's in his workshop now, making a new Earth, or something like it.

The old one is dead.

It's underwater, in case you forgot. The angels are said to be cleaning our lovely Earth, making it beautiful again. I'm pretty embarrassed about the whole thing. Out of the billions of souls that lived there, not one of us could clean up our mess. God is angry about that. He's locked us out of the Pearly Gates until we apologize for what we did to our home.

We're stuck.

I've been walking around outside for two-thousand years. So far, no one has figured out how to apologize. That was something else we never learned how to do on Earth.

I hope we learn soon. We aren't going anywhere unless God opens those Gates.

And I hope the angels clean up that big train station in Denver, Colorado. That's where my favorite bathroom is. It has been two-thousand years and seven days since I've seen it. I remember being on the toilet seat. It was cold against my bare skin. The tiled floor was sticky with urine. In front of me, the stall door had a message. It said in black marker:

"Hold my hand when the world ends."

I smiled at those words.
They were honest.
I was jealous that I hadn't thought of them myself.

The stall was decorated with all kinds of honesty. Next to me, someone had quoted the United States' Constitution. The words *"We the people"* were written inside of bombs. The bombs were being dropped out of a plane. The plane was flying over an old village.

Next to that was a drawing of a vagina. It was suspiciously accurate. I had seen only three vaginas in my life. One of those times was by accident.

I had a hard time believing a man could draw that vagina by memory.

***

I thought about masturbating in there.

It was my twenty-ninth birthday, and there was a roll of toilet paper by my feet.

Apparently, the janitors did not have the energy to hang that toilet paper. They didn't even have the energy to clean the floors.

Outside my stall, a television was playing. A news anchor was talking about huge, global storms within the next decade. He said something about pollution, and trash in the oceans. It was difficult to masturbate while the planet was dying.

I nudged the toilet paper with my shoe. It rolled out, sticking to the floor.

The television switched to a commercial. It was telling me which car to buy.

***

There was a bottle of medicine in my pocket. It was a prescription from the most honest man I knew, Dr. Daniel Abromovitz. We met once a week at his home in Boulder, Colorado. He had a little office where I sat down and told him about my brain.

My brain was full of monkey business back then. Full of voices that did not belong to me.

Didn't belong to anyone.

In the bathroom stall, the voices told me to jizz all over the tile floors.

Instead, I fingered that bottle of medicine from my pocket. Its label told me to swallow one tablet every six hours. The tablets were supposed to relax my brain. If I took them right, the voices in my head would disappear.

I popped the cap, unscrewed my water bottle.
With a small toast to Dr. Dan, I swallowed the pill.

***

I miss that magic medicine.

Each pill went a long way. They dropped down, dissolved, wrapped over my brain like cool towels. It all happened in a few seconds. Suddenly, there were no more voices. The urges were gone. I liked everything, and nothing made me sad. Back then, I was appreciating the bathroom graffiti.

I wanted to add something smart to the toilet stall, but nothing came out.

That's how it worked on Earth.

The creative people never knew when good stuff would pour out. The uncreative people never had anything.

That was me. I never had anything come out, even though I wanted to.

Instead, I admired bombs and villages.

I admired accurate vaginas.

***

Here is something important:

I spent an hour on the toilet seat.

With pants around my ankles, I daydreamed about rubbing my penis.

Part of me wanted to stay there forever. I was happy.

I remember the news came back on. It spoke about hurricanes again. But my brain was high on drugs. It wasn't worried about hurricanes. It wasn't worried about anything. To me, the end of the world was still inside all those novels I had read in high school. They were about aliens or fires or freezing to death.

Why did I get up? I could have stayed there and eaten pills for the rest of my life.

But there was a train waiting for me. It was going to roll up to the station soon. Then, it was going to roll all the way to San Francisco, California.

I think I stood up, pulled my pants around my waist.

"God bless America," I said, opening the stall door.

***

The far wall of the train station was paneled with huge windows. They went from floor to ceiling. They showed how beautiful *Mother* was. Of course, I tend to refer to planet Earth as Mother. I picked that up from someone who saved my life. He will be discussed, by and by.

Anyway, those windows were full of mountains and blue sky. The mountains looked small, being so far away. I closed one eye, and pinched my fingers together. It looked as though I could lift a mountain by its peak.

There were clouds, too. People always complained about them. They said blue skies were best. I always liked clouds though. They were floating over the mountains that day, looking like cotton candy with no flavor. They were getting fat with rain.

I found a seat by the giant windows. Mother was on the other side. I had no idea how angry she really was. I didn't care about her hurricanes. I never worried about all the trash in the ocean or the tortured atmosphere. My mind was on the train station itself. I remember how gray it looked. Everything was another shade of indifference. Not much went into making the place feel like home. The lights were stark and bright, meant for utility. People needed to see, and that was that.

Each wall was a naked slab of concrete. They were not as honest or artistic as the bathroom. They were cold. They had nothing to say to mankind. Only one scribble of graffiti had been tattooed on the wall next to me. It was a sentence written in yellow spray paint:

"Make love to the police."

I wished I had thought of that.

The ceiling in that place was very high. It almost looked black. Rafters were up there, hidden in shadow. I wonder now why that ceiling needed to be so tall. It seems like an awful waste of concrete. I remember thinking that birds might have lived up there. Maybe that's where God was hiding the whole time. No one would ever know.

If God was up there, I'm not surprised He never climbed down.

The floor was a mess.

It was more concrete, illustrated with chewing gum and old cigarettes. The trashcans were overflowing. I remember seeing a guy shove his hot dog into a trashcan. It fell out, landed on the concrete. No one cared.

Management was having a hard time cleaning up the place. I know that because I met the manager up here a while ago. We bumped into each other on our way to the Pearly Gates. We were both going to see if they had opened.

I asked him why that train station was so cold and dirty. He said the janitors all moved away. Apparently, they weren't satisfied with the pay, the hours, or even the job itself. He had told them, two-thousand years ago,

"That's what you get for being blue collar."

***

In that station, I spent a lot of time watching the people around me.

No one looked interested in a conversation.

That was fine. I didn't want to talk anyway. It was nice to sit down next to Mother and enjoy a cool towel over my brain. Plus, I had a chance to judge everyone. It was nice to invent lives for strangers. It was nice to give them problems.

I remember the woman sitting across from me.
I invented a big problem for her:
She hadn't been laid in forty years.

Her phone was getting abused. She was scrolling, tapping it hard. I thought her finger might break through. She was on social media, looking for the boy who took her virginity. Forty years prior, he must have said that he loved her. She must have believed him.

Now, all she had was a bad haircut and a cup of french fries in her lap. They were bleeding with all the ketchup in the world. She chewed with anger. I remember ketchup stuck to her lip.

The woman did not have a wedding ring. Instead, she wore an oversized purse. Inside, there was a bottle of antacids and a new vibrator. She also wore a tattoo on her arm. It was a poorly drawn feather. Inside the feather, it said in faded words, *"Be free."* The feather was breaking apart into a flock of birds. It was a very thoughtful tattoo.

This person had not had sex in forty years. During that time, I don't think she washed her hair once. It was a storm of red curls, frozen in place, splitting at the ends. That storm was tied up in a desperate bun. I wondered if there were ketchup and fries lost in there.

She had golden hoops dangling from her earlobes. They told everyone that she could afford to be classy and independent.

The hoops were plastic with gold paint.

***

Next to her was a man who weighed three-hundred pounds. His coronary arteries were filled with thick plaque. They were going to burst any second, giving him a heart attack.

I remember, too, that his shirt was dripping with sweat. I felt bad for his armpits. They were drowning. I also felt bad that he did not have a wedding ring, though I was not surprised. I imagined that he had been married three or four times, but crushed each of his wives trying to make love.

He was holding a photograph when I first saw him. His fat fingers looked like they came from a pack of hot dogs. I was surprised he didn't try to eat them.

But the man's biggest problem was that he was an asshole.

This was a problem I did not have to imagine. It would come to be true.

He would also become my friend.

***

I didn't feel bad about judging people any more.

Dr. Dan said it was normal. In fact, he said it was healthy.

I believe that.

It felt good to let the mind run wild, and exercise its own demons.

In that seat, waiting for the train, I opened my journal. It was full bad ideas and ugly drawings. I scribbled the two characters I just met. The red-haired, ketchup lady. The three-hundred pound man with hot dog fingers. They would be trapped in the journal. They would wait there until the end of time, destined to become a part of my novel.

That's why I created lives for people, after all.

That's why I was going to San Francisco, California.

I wanted to be a writer.

I wanted to be an author one day, with a journalist's background.

There was a job waiting for me at the Western Sun, the largest newspaper in California. On the phone, they said the starting pay for a journalist was barely above minimum wage. It was forty hours a week, and there was only one benefit: the company bathrooms were fabulously clean.

I didn't care about the pay. I had a trust fund worth five-hundred thousand dollars. The money landed under my name when I turned eighteen in human years. My father, who the money came from, had been dead for nineteen years. My mother, who no money came from, died thirty seconds later. They were killed in a double homicide and suicide. It happened in my childhood home in Oakland, California, two-thousand and nineteen years ago.

My mother found my father in bed with the nanny. The nanny was only eighteen in human years. Now, she is somewhere outside the Pearly Gates. I haven't found her yet. I wonder if her jaw is still missing.

My biological mother shot her through the mouth with a nine-millimeter pistol.

My father was shot through the eye. He tried to apologize first, attempting to save his own life. But humans were no good at apologizing.

Thirty seconds later, my mother put the gun to her own head.

She tried apologizing.

***

That was destined to be in my novel.

I wanted to make readers feel terrible. Why? I had no idea. These days, I realize Earthlings wanted to feel bad most of the time.

I felt bad about something I wrote in my journal:

"Thanks for dying."

It was a message for my father. I was thanking him for the relief that comes with a parent's death. I no longer felt guilty about becoming a journalist, and one day, an author. My father always looked down on those two ideas. He said they were not good ways to make over one-hundred thousand dollars a year.

My father made over one-hundred thousand dollars a year. He was the chief financial officer for a mid-level healthcare company in San Francisco, California. He went to work all day. I spent evenings and weekends and summer vacations with Roselle. Roselle was my eighteen year old nanny who had been shot in the face.

Before she died, she was my only friend.

After she died, I continued to write to her in my journal. I believed that, if I wrote hard enough, the words would find their way to Heaven.

I had no idea she was destined to be reincarnated.

That was my destiny too, and everyone else's.

I hope Roselle went back to Earth as something more innocent than a teenaged female.

I hope she was a deer that lived in a safe part of the woods.

***

And I wish I still had that journal.

It's in my pocket, somewhere back on Earth. Like everything else, it's underwater.

Anyway, back to the train station.

I was waiting to become a California journalist. I had finished staring at strangers, and was in the middle of writing another letter to Roselle.

I missed her every day.

I still do.

The letter said this:

Roselle, it's me again.

Today I turn twenty-nine. Here's a good gift idea: come to me in my dreams one night, and let me know if I've sent too many letters. I heard the post office in Heaven is always late. God regrets sending that memo which said, "Every day is a Sunday." He's missed a lot of important packages.

Anyway, I'm fine down here, thanks for asking. I got scared again, just now. Scared of writing. I told my dad that I was grateful for his death. I meant it. But I'm too much of a pussy to keep it in the journal. Dr. Dan, God bless him, thinks I have courage somewhere in me. He said there is an ocean of it. He said the best way to unleash it is to write exactly what I'm thinking. And of course, a few pills won't hurt.

Dr. Dan tells me the thoughts aren't my fault. They're not evil.
Apparently, everyone has voices now and then.
Everyone imagines themselves killing people, even if they don't want to.
That's how it's been for me.

Some days, my brain won't leave me alone. Tells me all kinds of non-sense. Just today, it told me to masturbate in public. In the past, it has told me to jump off bridges, drive my car into oncoming traffic.

But I never listen.
Those pills go a long way.

So it's been nineteen years. I still remember you the same way. I doubt God lets you have memories up there, not that you'd want them. Not after all that non-sense. But if you could, I bet you'd think of me the same way too. I was ten. I was at my worst. I still had fat from my baby years.

And yet, I had someone who thought I was pretty cool. Thanks.

So, which is it? Are you coming back, or waiting for me?
That first one might take a while, so hold tight.
I'll be there in a few.
I love you, Roselle.

***

I kissed the letter.

It was a stamp to get my note through the Pearly Gates, into her mailbox,

even on Sundays.

17

2

I FELL ASLEEP in that chair.

There was a good dream playing in my head, but it's gone now. Can't remember what it was, or who was in it.

That's another thing about the afterlife: memory dies fast. Dreams are the first to go. I have been walking around for two-thousand years. The rest of my thoughts are on their deathbed, or crawling in.

Anyway, a voice woke me up.

I was still sitting next to the windows. Mother was still outside, looking angry. Clouds were getting dark, rolling in fast.

The voice called again, blaring from loudspeakers:

"All aboard, last chance to climb on. Sweet Heavenly leaving in twenty minutes."

That was my train.

I don't know how I still remember those words. It has been two-thousand years since I heard them. They repeated a few more times, warning me to hurry up. So I gathered my things, got in line.

A man was waiting by the train doors. He was decorated in a navy blue suit that must have come from the President of the United States. It was dark and beautiful, untouched by dust. I believe it had a force field.

The man's cap was stamped with a brass plate. It had two laurels embossed in the metal. The word *"Conductor"* was etched in cursive letters. It could have been a big joke. At the time, I half believed God himself was standing in that suit, asking for my ticket. God had a warm, chocolate voice and irises made from exotic wood.

"Welcome aboard the Sweet Heavenly," he said, words melting through my face.

I was afraid of getting an erection.

"Thank you," I said back. I gave him my ticket, and moved on. It was quick. I was worried that if I stared too long at the gorgeous man, I might become a *faggot*. A faggot was a bundle of sticks used to start fires.

On planet Earth, I was an ordinary man.

Ordinary men often worried about becoming bundles of sticks.

***

There was a window seat onboard.

I sat next to Mother again, feeling her through the glass.

She was rainy, getting cold.

The train was cold too.

I had expected it to feel like the conductor's smile: warm and full of melted chocolate. His seat at the nose of the train must have been nice. I imagined it was decorated in leather and polished brass. There was a hot tub in there, and everything smelled like rich, deep coffee.

So I sat in the cold, unfolding my things. There was a pea coat, my backpack. I patted my pockets, feeling the familiar shape of the journal. I didn't have any keys to worry about, since I was officially homeless.

Back on Earth, one of our biggest fears was where we put our keys.

I didn't have any.

I was the richest homeless man in history.

There was more money in my bank account than in all the beggars' cups in the galaxy.

Prior to that day, I left my apartment in Denver, Colorado.

I knew I would miss that place.

It was a beautiful, high-rise penthouse in the mountains of a great state. That state was in the best country on Earth. Earth was the most treasured planet in the Milky Way. It had all the life in the Universe.

That's another thing you discover in the afterlife:

All life really did exist on Earth.

Everything had a human's soul, too.

Even the animals we killed back on Mother were stuffed with human souls.

I met Adolf Hitler yesterday. His soul is exactly four-thousand in human years. He came back as a flower. That flower had white petals and a fresh scent. It had been in the personal garden of some hippie in San Francisco, California.

I asked Adolf what he had been before he murdered everyone.

He said he had no idea.

He said he forgot about the murders.

Adolf was a nice soul.

But he was no good at apologizing.

***

Like I said, I was officially homeless.

I would sleep on the long ride. When I got off, I would sleep where I could. San Francisco was known for its unique citizens. They were always willing to share a bed.

At the time, that excited me.

Chemicals flushed through the tubes in my brain, reminding me how much fun I would have on the West Coast. I would be free. I would have a simple job with a simple life. I would ejaculate inside all different kinds of woman. They would be all different colors. Some would even have tattoos and metal piercings. I would grow vegetables in my small garden. Vegetarianism never seemed so responsible. Somehow, it would rain just enough on my garden. There would be enough produce for me, and all my neighbors. A family of immigrants to my left. A young couple to my right. Those two would be bartenders who sold artwork on the weekends. They would be covered in tattoos and *THC*. THC was tetrahydrocannabinol. It was illegal in the United States.

I smiled, penning my spoiled dream into the journal.

I wanted to show someone. They could see how much fun I was going to have. Everything else in the journal was a secret, however. I was worried someone might take my ideas and use them up. Mother was full of people that worried about plagiarism. Sometimes, the best ideas were never shared. Their creators were too worried about not getting credit.

I was a part of that demographic.

I hunched against the window, trying to write without an audience.

Looking back, I realize no one cared what I had to say, much less write.

***

My breath fogged the window.

In it, I drew a heart with my finger. Through my drawing, I could see the mountains so far away. If I was just a visitor on planet Earth, I might have thought they were the edge of the world.

I said that to myself over and over:

"The world, the world, the world, the world."

I put those words in my journal. They started to sound funny the more I said them. Underneath those words, I wrote that I really was just a visitor here.

"I've spent twenty-nine years on planet Earth..."

I wrote that in my journal too. It was trapped, as they say. My pen went on and on. It was scribbling carelessly, writing a story about human mortality.
This was it:

Mother had been circling in space for millions of years. One day, humans were born. One day, they died. Somewhere in the middle, they masturbated too much. They used up all the electricity looking for online pornography.
In our aftermath, God arranged LED lights on the dark side of the moon. From a distance, they spelled out a sentence:

"We tried."

It was mankind's tombstone. God always knew the dark side of the moon would come in handy for something like that. It allowed all the aliens who passed by to feel sadness. They might even learn a lesson about masturbation and the fate of the universe.

I smiled at my story. Back then, I thought it was clever.
I was glad the world was dying.
It gave me lots of content to shove inside my novel.

***

A suitcase plopped into the seat next to me.
I looked up.
It was the three-hundred pound man.

"Good morning," I said, "business or pleasure?" I don't know why I asked that. Like most people, much of what I said came from movies or television.

The guy didn't look at me. He was wrestling with himself, trying to remove a jacket. It could have been glued on.

He sat, wiping sweat from his face.

"The name's Bulgruf," he said, breathing with his whole body. "Doctor Bulgruf."

"A pleasure, Doctor Bulgruf. I'm Hopeman."

My eyes were being sucked into his stomach.

It rose and fell with each breath, as if the man's body were two giant lungs.

"Yes," he said.

"Pardon?"

"You asked if I was here for business."

I paused

"Oh yes," I said, looking at his neck. I thought it was a pack of hotdogs. "What kind of business calls you to California?"

He looked at me like I had just asked him to pull down his pants.

"Science."

I waited for some elaboration.

There would be none. He was going for science, and that was that.

It was fine. I didn't want to talk anyway. I was trying to organize a novel.

We sat in silence for a while. It was peaceful. We could have driven off a cliff, and in that moment, I would be at peace. Dr. Dan's magic medicine was doing good work. My brain was cool. It was cool enough for me to write again. I was outlining my story about masturbation and the fate of the universe.

Though I never got far.

My new companion suddenly wanted to talk.

"I'm going to a conference," Bulgruf said to me.
"Is that right?"
"Yes. A big conference. Scientists from all over, coming to discuss the ocean. Storms are brewing, you know. A lot is going down."
"Sounds interesting," I said, doodling my ideas. I was pretending to listen.
"You're goddamn right it's interesting," he said. "You do know the world is in trouble, yes?"
I dropped my pen, closed the journal.
"Sorry," I said, "come again?"
Bulgruf was livid. His face was swollen with heat.
"Maybe I can tag along," I asked. "Might be fun."
"Are you a scientist? You look like you're in high school."
"No sir," I said, "not a scientist. Just a man on a train."

Bulgruf laughed at that. He said to me, waving his hand, "We'll be better off without. You'd get lost on your way inside."
I looked him in the face, and said,
"Please, daddy, I'll be good."

***

I've had two-thousand years of hindsight to learn from. What it's telling me now is this:

"I almost got punched in the face."

Bulgruf wanted throw his fist into my nose.
What saved me was the train. It started rumbling to life, warming up whatever motivation it had left. It was an old train. I don't think it should have been operating any more. But from somewhere below, the engines rumbled like two machines fighting or making love.

Bulgruf never hit me. My sarcasm was killed by the growling beneath.

Also, I met Bulgruf up here the other day, outside the Pearly Gates. He told me that was his first time on a train. He thought it was going to explode.

I told him the same thing.

It was true, I was scared. I was afraid that I'd never be able to publish a novel, since I would soon explode. Bulgruf was afraid he would never read a textbook again.

We both agreed about wanting to punch each other.

***

The train shot forward.

Everything was light. My heart felt like a fish, flopping in my chest.

I closed my eyes, trying to relax.

Suddenly, I believed in God. I was praying to him that we would be ok. My prayer was for everyone on the train, since I didn't want to seem selfish.

Bulgruf's neck jiggled. His briefcase was clenched over his heart.

"It's ok," I said, to him. "I've been on trains a thousand times—

"Silence."

He cut my sentence in half. He didn't care.

The man looked at me, and said,

"I don't need a fool's advice."

The train was going faster.

It was about to explode.

I was clenching my journal.

I could feel my stomach sweating, or bleeding. It might have been sliding out my asshole.

***

Then it stopped.

Suddenly, everything was smooth.

The rumbling died. It was light, even comforting. Looking out the windows, the mountains were moving behind us gently. Trees and clouds rolled away as the train soothed over its tracks.

It felt like the engine was drenched in warm butter.

I forgot to thank God for saving my life.

Then, the conductor's voice came over the train speakers:

"Alright, folks, the train has reached its maximum speed. It is now safe to leave your seats. The attendants will be by shortly. Have a comfortable and relaxing ride."

I melted in his chocolate.

I didn't even care if I was a faggot. It was good to be alive.

***

About hindsight again: it tells me I was ashamed of myself. It tells me Bulgruf was ashamed of himself.

We didn't speak for a while after that.

We both almost shit in our pants.

I'm imagining the scenario now: Two grown men, sitting beside each other. Both with poop in their underwear. We were on our way to San Francisco, California, with loaded pants.

And somehow, I was going to sleep with many exotic women.

I remember looking at Bulgruf. He was still nervous.

I said to him,

"Jesus, I didn't expect that."

The scientist was putting a nitroglycerin tab under his tongue. He thought he might be having a heart attack.

I congratulated myself. I knew he had a heart problem.

***

So we sat in silence. It hung between us like a deep fog.
I decided to rebuild.

On Earth, trauma had a way of tearing everything down, so it could be made stronger.

I asked him,

"So what kind of scientist are you?"

Bulgruf shook his head.

"The kind that saves the world," he said, sprinkling his fingers. His sarcasm was as good as mine. I laughed to be friendly.

"How's that going?" I asked. It seemed like the conversation was already on its deathbed, but I wasn't giving up yet.

Bulgruf closed his eyes and said,

"Don't bother. You would not understand."

***

I shook my head, writing into my journal. I scribed a message to Bulgruf, telling him to *"not bother eating for the next year, you fat piece of shit."*

It was a very mature thing to say.

"Sorry," I said to him. "It's just that, well, I've never met a real scientist before."

Bulgruf turned to me and said,

"Don't be smart with me, you sarcastic, young fool."

I was shocked. I never knew how foolish I was.

"Fist me, doctor," I said.

Bulgruf was livid.

He stood up, pointed his finger right in my face, and said, "Listen, you little bitch. Everything you have is from people like me. Every drop of creativity, every moment of civilized prosperity you enjoy, comes from the thinkers. It comes from science. We build greatness, you take it for granted."

He shoved his way down the aisle, turning back for a moment.

"You are welcome for this life of luxury, you little shit."

***

Hindsight tells me I could have avoided all that.

I probably would have been less sarcastic if I knew I was going to die in seven days.

Bulgruf might have been more patient if he knew he was going to die in seven days.

I closed my eyes after he left. My journal had been abused enough already. Parts of my brain were holding onto Bulgruf's words, putting them back together. I replayed that conversation over and over, thinking about everything we did wrong.

Inside my mouth, a few words kept rolling around.

They tasted funny.

"The world, the world, the world, the world."

3

As I said, Bulgruf and I saw each other a while ago, right outside Heaven.

He was trying to figure out how to apologize to God.

He was like everyone else.

I gave him a hug, told him that I'd missed him.

There is no Hell by the way. Not that I know of.

Outside of Heaven is nice though. Clouds as far as you can see. They aren't water vapor. They are made of some kind of aether, some mystical plasma. It floats around like mist. I'm stepping on it. It's above, beneath, and all around me. It feels like walking through an open field on the foggiest morning ever.

That's only if you're bored, of course. That's if nothing else is on your mind.

If you think hard enough about something, the clouds will become your imagination. It's true. You can project your thoughts onto the aether. They are very sensitive to human brainwaves. So, if you think really hard, you almost feel like you are back on Mother.

For most of us, our only memories are from our last life. Who knows how many years we've all been alive or how many times we've been reincarnated. Hitler only remembers being a flower, after all. I think that's nice.

Right now, the aether clouds are surrounding me.

I'm in my childhood home in Oakland, California.

Bulgruf is here too.

We are sitting in my living room, talking about the time we met.

Sometimes I ask him to think deeply, so we can relax in one of his memories. He is an interesting man, full of places and stories.

Bulgruf usually changes the subject.

He's not fond of his memories.

He tells me that, after our argument, he went to the back of the train. Apparently, Bulgruf regrets all the aggression. He regrets a lot of things.

The man was an environmental scientist back on Earth. He was employed by different agencies to reverse our planet's pollution.

That was difficult. During our lifetime, Mother was avalanching towards death.

I died in the year two-thousand and sixteen.

So did Bulgruf and Mother.

Bulgruf started as a scientist in the year nineteen seventy-five.

That gave him forty-one years to save Mother.

Right now we're in my imagination, in my living room, in Oakland, California. Bulgruf is telling me that, on the train so long ago, he thought about apologizing to me. He wanted to die one day knowing he could apologize. He didn't think he'd ever done it before.

Back then, we were both looking out train windows. Bulgruf was seeing everything go backwards, just like I was. He saw the mountains melt away as the train rolled past. This got him thinking about time travel. He thought if the train went fast enough, it might be able to break through time and land in the future.

Or he could go backwards.

Bulgruf would know what to do differently, the second time around. He would know when to speak up, and when to remain silent. He would know when to sell his stocks, what lottery numbers were best.

He would know what was most important in the world.

Bulgruf would know that, no matter what he did, the world was going to end in forty-one years.

***

The scientist sat across from me in my childhood home in Oakland, California.

He was in the chair my father used to sit in. If my father were here now, he'd be looking at us with one eye. The other was blown out by a nine-millimeter bullet.

"That's her," Bulgruf said. He was thinking hard, focusing his mind.

An image manifested in my living room. It floated there, on cloud-aether, projecting from Bulgruf's memories.

It was a woman's face.

She had a long, gray scarf hanging from her shoulders. It was frayed at the ends and pocked with holes.

Bulgruf said her name was Mayla.

He told me their story.

4

THE FOLLOWING is an honest account, according to Bulgruf, a human being from planet Earth:

Mayla was his true love.

She was a librarian at the college Bulgruf attended back in nineteen seventy-five. Mayla saw him in the library every day, looking through the same textbooks. He was very handsome back then. The man was twenty-five in human years, tall, and trim. He had high cheekbones.

Mayla noticed all that. It made her wet with chemicals. And she noticed which books he rented. They were usually about oceans, and not the kind with nice pictures. The man was trying to understand how they worked, why they were getting so full of trash.

One day, after he returned the books, Mayla slipped a few of her poems within the pages. There was no reason for that. It was what she did to all the non-fiction books in the library. Mayla stuffed hand-made poetry inside, trying to animate those boring tomes. Her poems were all written on strips of wrinkled parchment, scribed with cursive letters.

Mayla was also twenty-five in human years. She had nice breasts and high cheekbones. In her time on Earth, she gathered a beautiful vocabulary. It came from all the stories she read. Well, she used that vocabulary to write beautiful stories of her own.

They were never published.

But still, Bulgruf got to read them. He eventually rented those textbooks again.

He was the only one who ever did.

***

The next day, Bulgruf stomped back into the library.

He threw his book onto the service desk, demanding to know,

"What the hell is this?"

The man's finger was pointed at a pile of wrinkled parchment.

Mayla looked him in the eyes.

She said,

"I'm sorry sir, may I help you?"

"Yes," Bulgruf replied, "go ahead and explain this pile of shit." His armpits were drowning. The man's face was swollen with heat.

Mayla stood. She had nice breasts and high cheekbones.

"I'm sorry, sir," she said, "what seems to be the problem?"

Bulgruf was livid. He hated her.

But he also was getting an erection.

"Sir," Mayla said, "I'd be glad to put you in touch with our manage—"

"Silence."

He cut her sentence in half.

"I don't need a fool's advice. I want an explanation."

Mayla thought he was gorgeous when he was angry.

Still, she leaned over the service desk, getting close to his face.

She said,

"Go fuck yourself."

***

Later that night, Bulgruf went home and did as he was told.

He ejaculated all over his bathroom floor.

There were no accurate vaginas on the wall, no honest graffiti.

So, he used his imagination.

He thought of Mayla.

Before leaving the library, he had taken the book, and one last glance at that bitch.

There was a tattoo on her collarbone.

It said in black ink,

"Fly".

***

Bulgruf's memory has faded an awful lot since his time on Mother. But he remembers enough. He told me about opening his textbook, getting back to work with a clear head. I think all his anger shot out with that semen.

So, Bulgruf took a deep breath, and opened the book.

He paused.

He could not believe what he saw.

In the crease, there was yet another poem.

"Motherfucker," he said, lifting the parchment as if it was a dead bug.

Bulgruf paused, looking at the poem.

He read the whole thing.

It was not a poem.

It was a phone number.

***

That number turned into a phone call. It went unanswered. Bulgruf did not realize he tried to use it at four o' clock in the morning. He had a hard time sleeping that night, the way men did when they thought about women.

Then, Bulgruf woke up to a phone call.
It was the librarian.
That call turned into an awkward conversation. Neither of them apologized for what happened.
Instead, they found a square on the calendar.
Both people, scientist and fool, agreed to meet at the library that upcoming weekend, and make up.
It was the last day of school, and the first day of summer vacation.

***

Summer vacation was a good time for Americans.
Ice cream cones were in season, and everyone got matching tattoos.
The tattoos said things like *"fly away,"* or *"coexist."*

Summertime was very persuasive. It made people wet, or full of semen. It convinced young people that they would live forever.
Bulgruf and Mayla were both twenty-five in human years, and horny.
They both had apartments very close to each other.
That turned into walks around town.
Walks turned into late night conversations. During all those conversations, nothing important was ever said. In fact, they didn't even listen to the words. The sound of each other's voice was a good song, all by itself.
Good songs turned into sleepovers.
Sleepovers turned into love-making.

One night, Bulgruf and Mayla made love on a picnic blanket in the woods. It was a quilt she made out of old tee shirts. They threw it over a grass field, deep in the trees. There were no trails, no paths. The two love birds flew there by accident, and made a nest.

The lovebirds orgasmed.

The lovebirds held each other for a while, watching outer space get sprinkled with stars.

Orgasms and outer space did a lot for people.
They made it easy to be honest.

So the two human beings said honest things for the rest of the night. They talked about the future. Mayla was going to be a successful artist. Her paintings were going to be in galleries all over the world, or in rich people's homes. She would also finally publish that poetry. Bulgruf was going save the world. He told his lover that when fall came, he would have an opportunity to work in a famous research lab in the Andes Mountains.

It was true.

He said that if it all worked out, he would be offered a job there.

"What do you think?" He asked. Fireflies were waking up, poking the air with soft light.

Mayla got up, sifted through her bag.

"I think," she said, "you'll need some of this before you go."

She was holding a joint.

***

That summer, Bulgruf and Mayla ran away together every night. The fireflies watched them make love, saw them take photographs. The photos all turned out horrible. The lighting was off. Neither lover was any good with a camera. Only one picture survived. It was Mayla staring through the camera, haloed by sunset. She had an old scarf hanging from her neck. It was full of holes and frayed ends. It seemed to say, *"Follow me into the woods."*

The fireflies heard them say honest things all night.

Something about her going to the mountains with him. Something about never being apart. The fireflies heard Bulgruf say, *"Yes."*

"Do you mean it?"
"Of course."

Bulgruf inhaled from the joint, its end glowing bright red.

He wondered if there was anyone else in outer space. And if they were up there, he wondered if they had fallen in love. The scientist, high on chemicals, wondered if love existed anywhere else in the universe.

Bulgruf inhaled, the joint glowing bright red.

He wondered if anyone could see the little fire from so far away.

5

I ASKED BULGRUF if he took her to the mountains.
He said he did not.

On September 1, nineteen seventy-five, he left Mayla in the middle of the night to get in a car. That car drove to the airport. The airport led to a plane. That plane was going to Argentina, where Bulgruf would be a student researcher. The lab was high in the Andes Mountains.

***

She was asleep when he left her.
They spent the night in her room, watching a thunderstorm.
Mayla had an apartment just off campus. It was cheap, and entirely concrete. Three oriental rugs and a mattress covered the cold floors. The rugs were from her parents, who bought them in India. They, like most young people, wanted to be world travelers. So the couple spent most of their twenties roaming Europe and Asia. They brought back three oriental rugs, artwork, and a pregnant uterus.
A life of adventure had become another relic for them, something swallowed by the past.

Nothing stimulated them any more.

After Mayla was born, they had no time to be young again. It was too expensive.

Heroin was not expensive.

At twenty-seven in human years, Mayla's parents overdosed on cheap narcotics.
Mayla was one, in human years.

***

Bulgruf knew all this when he stared down at her, his plane ticket in hand. He knew that she loved him, and would give everything to him.

It was the autumn of nineteen seventy-five, and a snowstorm was falling from outer space. Somehow, snow came early that year.

He looked at his woman. She was asleep on a mattress.
His neurons were telling him to *"Run. The plane is waiting. Get in the car."*
His heart was telling him how warm it must be in those blankets.

The room was silent and dark.
If there had been light, Bulgruf would see homemade art on the walls. Mayla sold it in local galleries. That helped her afford a concrete apartment.
His brain told him, *"There is no room for art in the Andes lab. You'll never get work done."*
His heart was running out of things to say.

***

Years went by.

Bulgruf performed well in the Andes Mountains. The people up there wanted him to stay, in exchange for one-hundred thousand dollars a year.

He agreed.

Bulgruf stayed for a long time, in fact. He eventually became the lead researcher for that lab. Scientists all over the globe requested his help. He was an expert in oceanography, climate change, and so on. The man worked on solutions every day, looking for new ways to protect the planet. He even tried to use Earth's natural motions for alternative energy.

He didn't know it, but Mother was already doomed.

There was nothing he could do to save her.

Bulgruf was also doomed.

He died forty-one years after going to the Andes Mountains.

And for forty-one years, Bulgruf carried a photograph in his pocket.

It was a picture of a woman, trapped in nineteen seventy-five. She was wearing sunlight, and an old scarf.

6

BULGRUF left me too.

He gave me a hug, said it was nice to see a friend make it so close to Heaven.

I told him the same.

Then, Bulgruf walked away, looking in every direction.
I think he was searching for the librarian.

***

That was good poetry.
I wish I had thought of it.

And I wish I had a bathroom stall to write it in.

The cloudscape outside Heaven is mostly gray. Not much goes into making the place feel like home. I've been trying to imagine home for two-thousand years now. Every time I concentrate, I forget what Earth looks like, just a little bit.

Two millennia is a long time for memory to last.
I don't blame it for dying.

I don't think I know what Roselle looks like either.

By the time I was twenty-nine in human years, I had no idea what my biological mother looked like. She splattered her brain against the closet doors in my childhood home in Oakland, California.

I thanked God for a closed-casket funeral.

***

I have very little idea what my father looks like.
We might have passed each other up here, on our way to apologize to God.

Speaking of which, I went to the Pearly Gates recently. I looked at them. They really are made of pearl. I scratched the bars to see if any paint would come off.
It did not.
It's real pearl.

White mist floats through the bars. It comes out so thick, you can't see through. I wonder what that is all about.
Anyway, I told God something which I thought would get his attention.
I looked up at the Gates, and said,

"Hold my hand when the world ends."

It did not work.
Nothing happened.
It was the most honest thing I could think of. Still, I suppose it was something I had plagiarized from two-thousand years ago.

My next idea was to draw a very accurate vagina.

***

Back to the train.

It was where I met the most beautiful woman I can remember. She came walking down the aisle. Her thin body was hanging with sweatpants and a hoodie. I imagined how easy it would be to take those clothes off.

During our last moments on Earth, we left on a good note. The two of us died together, after all. Dying with another human being is a very special thing. I guess they call it bonding.

But we were not always so close.

I am still ashamed at how it all started.

***

"Mind if I sit here?" She asked, looking down at me through dark sunglasses.

I told her it was no problem at all.

I was busy trying to conceal my erection. Men spent most of their lives pretending they were not erect.

I said, "Nice weather, right?"

I regretted that question. It was boring. I was boring.

There was no reason for me to ask that.

"Very nice," she said. At the time, I was disgraced that a beautiful woman with high cheekbones did not digest my sarcasm. The weather was cold and horrible.

So silence settled between us.

Hindsight is telling me that I should have been quiet.

But I spoke.

"The name's Hopeman, by the way. Nice to meet you."

"Flyes," she said back.

"Interesting name," I said.

There was silence. I waited for something to happen.

But, that was that.

Her name was Flyes.

It no longer mattered what my name was: I was inside a coffin of embarrassment. I had shrunk under the inability to ask good questions.

I tried again.

"So," I said, "where are you headed?"

There was more silence.

Flyes was pretending to be asleep.

That's what hindsight tells me.

I wanted a meteoroid to crash into Earth and destroy everyone. Only then would my shame vanish.

We sat without words for a long time.

Beneath us, the train engine rumbled softly.

It sounded like two machines making love.

***

I saw Flyes up here a while ago, outside the Gates.

She hugged me.

I thanked God for not having a penis any more.

That's another thing about this place: you lose your penis on the way up. Just disappears. That will be discussed, by and by.

Anyway, Flyes asked how I had been, said it was tough to be social up here.

She was right.

There are billions of souls waiting for Heaven to open up. That seems like a lot, but God's front yard is endless. Like I said, everything is aether clouds as far as you can see. Every soul is wandering around, looking for God, or something to do. It's very easy to get lost. Sometimes, I have no idea where I am. Sometimes, I won't see another soul for weeks. Flyes and I agreed that it is safe to stay close to the Gates.

She told me about finding some strangers a while back. They were lost, but Flyes showed them the way back to the Pearly entrance.

It was a group of four men. On Mother, they had been the most famous band of all time. It was no coincidence that Flyes had been a fan. Still is.

I wish I had thought of their songs.

But they are over there now, talking with Flyes. She's lovely, and they all seem fabulously charismatic.

Still, I take pride in knowing something those guys don't.

I know the scars on Flyes' feet are from broken glass.

7

Two-thousand years ago, I met the bitchiest angel God ever made. She had high cheekbones, and was going to San Francisco, California. I still think about how easy it would have been to peel those loose clothes from her body and make love to her.

Her name was Flyes.

She was pretending to be asleep so I would stop talking.

These were the only two things I knew about her: She had a name, and she wanted me to shut up.

I was somehow closer to her than any living woman.

Hindsight tells me that chemicals in my brain were causing a lot of problems.

Dr. Dan said that sex hormones had a way of screwing up my balance. They encouraged the thoughts, voices, and so on. He thought it was an excellent idea to masturbate, and then take pills.

"But not in public," he would say with a laugh, *"no rubbin' your ducky in public."*

Apparently, a lot of his patients did that.

So I kept my word. I never once ejaculated around other people, not even in the most honest bathroom stall in the world.

***

I certainly didn't stroke my penis on a train next to a beautiful woman.

Soon, that woman fell asleep for real.
She curled up into a ball, the way cute, petite women did when they were sleepy on long rides.
Her shoes fell off.

I paused, staring at her feet.
Her soles were a network of leathery scars.
I looked at her fingers. No wedding ring. No jewelry at all.

My brain was drunk on bad chemicals, telling me that she had been raped.
They told me the scars were from abuse.
She had been abused, tortured, raped. The rest of her body was probably covered in scars too, and filled with semen. Her abuser wanted to punish every cell in Flyes' body.
I didn't write her character into my novel. It was too brutal, and I was being a pussy. So, my imagination drooled over Flyes' feet.

Dr. Dan was right. The voices were growling.
They said,
"She was raped relentlessly, over and over. You could rape her too if you ripped those clothes from her weak body."

A boulder of guilt sank through me.
So I fished out the pills, opened my water bottle.

One piece of magic medicine, down the hatch.

***

After that, my brain was cool.
I had no more urges. No voices.
Everything was light and peaceful.
I was able to look at Flyes and appreciate her little details. The pills told me she had a wonderful personality.

In real life, she was a sarcastic bitch.
Hindsight says that's why we got along so well.
Dying together wasn't so bad.

***

As I said, we met up here the other day.
I was complaining to her that none of my friends invited me into their imaginations.
She told me I needed friends first.

Anyway, we talked about the time we met.
It was a little fuzzy in our minds, but we tried. Our imaginations worked together to recreate the scene: the train, the frosty windows, her pretending to be asleep.

Aether clouds swirled around us, reflecting what it all looked like.
I smiled at how real it was.

***

Flyes asked me if I would have still gotten on that train if I knew the world was about to end. I told her I didn't know.
That was honest.
I think I would have stayed in bed until water crashed through my high-rise apartment in Denver, Colorado.
That really would have happened.
North America was pummeled by waves three miles high. I don't know exactly what happened to everyone else.

Flyes said she might have killed herself instead of getting on the train.

To me, that was silly. I never understood how people had the balls to put a gun to their own heads. But, my biological mother did it. Maybe it ran in the family.

Flyes said she would have overdosed on something, not used a gun. She sounded very serious. I didn't make any jokes. I knew she had been a veteran drug user back on Earth.

***

Flyes said she did not want to invite me into her memories because there was nothing I would like.

I insisted.

By then, we were sitting across from each other on my bed in Oakland, California. I was showing her my life.

It was the bed where Roselle tucked me in. It was the bed where I woke up to the sound of gunshots. It was the bed that I crawled back into after dialing the police.

I went on, telling her everything that happened. We were surrounded by the aether clouds in God's front yard.

Flyes said she was sorry about all that.

I said it was her turn.

She warned me.

Flyes said everything in her past life was full of narcotics, blood, and semen.

I told her we might be up here for a while.

8

THE FOLLOWING is an honest account, according to Flyes. She was a human from planet Earth, just like me. This is how she ended up on the train.

***

Her mother called her a bitch.

Flyes was ten years old, standing with her back against the refrigerator door. Behind that door, there was no food. In front, there was a little girl with a knife pointed at her face.

It demanded to know where the drugs were.

Apparently, her mother worked all week to get fresh heroin. Flyes was accused of stealing it. She was ten, in human years.

Her mother spit in Flyes' face.

"I know you took it for yourself, you little bitch."

Flyes tried to explain. She even apologized, which she was no good at.

Her mother slapped Flyes across the face.

Then the tears came, and more apologies.

Flyes was on her knees.

Her mother was screaming. She ripped open the cabinets, threw everything out. Plates and bowels crashed, shattering.

Somehow, Flyes passed out.

Her brain had sympathy. It knocked her asleep to avoid more trauma.

She fell limp on the linoleum floor.

When Flyes woke up, it was nighttime. She was all alone in her childhood home, surrounded by broken glass. It was a cold apartment in Golden, Colorado. There were two mattresses, one bedroom, one bathroom. The kitchen and living room shared the same space. The sink was full of dirty plates. They had not been cleaned in weeks. There had not even been food in two days.

Flyes' mother made two-thousand dollars a month. She had a very popular vagina, and used it to pay for food, rent, and narcotics. That food eventually became more narcotics.

Flyes crawled under her mother's blanket, smelled her pillow. It was covered in cheap perfume and cigarette smoke.

There was one window in the bedroom, covered by a dark blue tapestry. A streetlight glowed somewhere outside.

When her mother was in a good mood, she would tell Flyes the story about how she got that tapestry. It involved hitchhiking somewhere in Portland, Oregon. There was a hobo, a bag of fake dollar bills. Somehow, a police chase fit in there too.

The girl closed her eyes. They were dripping with tears. She whispered something, hoping her words might float away and find her mother:

"I love you."

***

Four years later, the girl ran away from her foster home in Boulder, Colorado. She had been placed there by the decision of social services.

Flyes was fourteen in human years when she escaped that orphanage. She had been molested in her room every night by the groundskeeper. He and his wife kept the young girls in a closed-off wing of the building, for which there was only one key.

Somehow, the groundskeeper lost that key. It was what all people did: lost their keys. Flyes found it, opened the door, left. It was the easiest way to escape. She walked right out the front door without a sound.

That night she slept in a junkyard that had been abandoned for twenty years. It was full of old, American muscle cars that had rusted their way into the afterlife. One of them still had windows and leather seats. Its front end was destroyed.

Somehow the door was unlocked.

Flyes crawled in.

For a moment, before falling asleep, she thought she smelled perfume and cigarettes.

***

The girl became sixteen, in human years.

She survived by sucking men's penises. Men all over Boulder would pay her to come into gas station bathrooms, and have their penises sucked. Her customers knew she was only sixteen. No one cared. A mouth on the penis was similar to affection, which was hard to find on planet Earth.

She was given fifty dollars per penis.

Flyes, at sixteen years old, had a full-time job.

One time, she gave a blow job to the manager of a movie theater. It was in the janitor's closet. Afterwards, he gave her fifty dollars, and his nickname. It was Big Carlos.

Big Carlos told Flyes that she could be making one-hundred thousand dollars a year if she *"Put that pretty little mouth to work"*. The manager said he was going to quit his job, and *"Make my own company."*

Sixteen year old females were not known for their foresight.

Flyes agreed to make that much money.

***

By twenty-five in human years, Flyes was rich. She was now earning a hundred dollars per penis. Big Carlos made even more than that. He was the manager of over twenty girls, all of them with popular mouths.

Still, Flyes was his favorite. He called her his *main bitch*. It was a term of endearment. Big Carlos told Flyes that, since he kept her employed, she owed him favors whenever he asked. Apparently, he needed to molest her every night.

So, on her off hours, Flyes was made into a semen disposal machine. Big Carlos raped her in every way he could imagine. Eventually, she was not allowed to leave his penthouse in Boulder, Colorado. He told her that if she was ever caught trying to escape, he would *"Put a bullet in that pretty little mouth."*

That would kill her.

Worse, she would be out of a job.

***

Flyes spent three months indoors.

She was trapped in Big Carlos' penthouse with nothing to do but shave her vagina. It was how her manager liked it. The woman was trying to avoid a bullet in her mouth.

One day, she noticed that Big Carlos left his house keys on the kitchen table.

He was like most people. He always lost his keys.

Flyes took them, opened the door.

She paused.

There was Big Carlos, standing outside his own front door, looking for his house keys.

***

He pushed Flyes into the refrigerator, slapped her across the face.

"You like that, you fucking bitch?" He said. Big Carlos threw a bottle of liquor against the floor. It smashed into millions of sharp flakes. He threw another bottle, then another.

Flyes was trying to apologize. She was crying, curled up against the refrigerator.

Big Carlos pointed a gun to her head.
He told her,
"Get up, bitch."

She obeyed. Flyes stood, staring at the floor. Her knees were shaking. Big Carlos escorted her from the kitchen, into the living room.

"Stop right there," he said. He held the muzzle of a forty-five caliber revolver against the back of her skull.

In front of her was a trail of broken bottles leading to the front door. They were in puddles of rum and vodka.

He clicked the pistol's hammer.
"Walk, bitch."

Flyes tried apologizing. She peed, fear and urine leaking out of her.

He pushed her head with the pistol.
"You want to leave me? Then fucking walk."

9

I ASKED HER what happened next.

Flyes told me that she could not walk for weeks after that. She thought she was going to bleed out, or die of an infection. She guessed the alcohol killed all the bacteria.

Big Carlos hand-cuffed her to a bed post.
He continued to rape her for weeks.
One night he stumbled in drunk, a bottle of whiskey in hand.

After he fell asleep, Flyes took the bottle, broke it.
She cut his throat open with broken glass.
It took Big Carlos seventeen seconds to die.

The handcuff keys were in his pocket.

She unlocked herself.
Flyes took her time with a luxurious shower, changed into sweatpants and a hoodie. She put thousands of dollars in cash inside her purse.
Then, the woman walked right out the front door, landed in a taxi cab.
That taxi took her to the train station in Denver, Colorado.
She was going anywhere.

***

Her memory had made it full circle.

We imagined the train together. Then, Flyes took us to the kitchen in her childhood home. Then the orphanage, which lead to the backseat of an old, American muscle car. We stopped for a moment in the janitor's closet of a movie theater. That took us to a penthouse in Boulder, Colorado. Then, back on the train.

The aether clouds faded. The train slowly melted away, turning into gray mist.

We were back in God's front yard.

Eventually I spoke up.

I asked Flyes if she remembered her mother's face.

She said no.

All she could remember was a tattoo on her mother's collarbone.

It said, in faded black ink,

"Fly."

10

FLYES LEFT ME soon after that.

She gave me a hug, then walked away to join her new friends. They were singing old songs, the ones they invented back on Earth.

I was alone in the clouds again.

Part of me felt bad for insisting that Flyes dredge up her memories.

I guess some things never change.

I still enjoy other people's problems.

***

On Mother, I got very lucky.

I didn't have many problems. My first real problem was Roselle getting shot in the mouth.

The next time I had a problem, I was asleep for the whole thing.

In fact, I was asleep next to the most beautiful woman I could imagine.

We shared a train together.

It exploded.

***

Two-thousand years ago, the United States of America was home to the largest church in the world. It was called the Global Church of the Almighty Creator. It was a radical division of Christianity. Eventually, the Church got so popular, it broke off to form its own religion. It had a billion followers across the planet. Their capital cathedral was in San Francisco, California.

The High Priest resided there. His name was Arthur Sullenous.

Every Sunday, he preached about the second coming of the Creator.

The world, at the time, was dying fast.

His believers thought this was a sign of divine apocalypse. They believed that mankind was pissing off the Creator with all its technological antics.

The believers were so passionate, that every day after sermon, they would march around outside the church, praying loudly. They held signs that said, *"God will destroy you,"* and *"Hell is waiting for you."*

One time, a homeless man was making his way to a soup kitchen. He crossed the church plaza just as it was filling up with believers. Apparently, the hobo lingered for too long. He wasn't joining in prayer. The people surrounded him, demanding an explanation as to why he was being such a nuisance. He was called a terrorist and an opponent of free speech.

When he did not reply, insults turned into fists.

He was pummeled for one minute and thirty-six seconds. That was how long it took to crack the vertebrae in his neck.

Apparently, he was blind and deaf from World War II.

***

It was those same disciples who placed a homemade explosive device on the train tracks leading into San Francisco,

California. They wanted to keep everyone out. Trains might be carrying a lot of sinners, after all.

> Sweet Heavenly rolled right over that device.
> It exploded immediately.

> I was asleep, so I don't remember what it felt like.
> My brain had a lot of sympathy.

11

THAT TRAIN CRASH back in two-thousand sixteen was, at the time, the largest act of domestic terrorism in the United States.

Yet, the disciples in San Francisco would soon top their own title. In the following six days, they would kill a total of thirty-thousand human beings.

***

But, at the time, I survived an American milestone.
It was something to put in my novel.

Another thing I would include in my novel was an unsuspecting hero. Earth was a great place for heroes. There were always tragedies. Tragedies made heroes out of ordinary men.

I would make sure my book had plenty of tragedy.

Anyway, my hero would be based on the man who saved my life. His name was Henry LaFelle.

In his last life as a human, LaFelle was in the shape of an old farmer. I saw him the other day, lying down in a patch of white clouds. He seemed to be doing fine. The man was still old, I think in his fifties. He looked just like the farmer I remember.

That's something else I forgot to mention: up here, people look like they did just before they died. Same clothes and everything.

If I ever see Roselle, she will be naked.
So will my father.

***

LaFelle and I talked for a long time the other day.
I asked if he knew a way inside.

"Inside where?" He asked.
"Heaven. Where else?" I asked.
He closed his eyes, thinking hard.
"Don't know nothin' about that," he said. "I thought we were already there."

LaFelle was having a nice time. Apparently, he had no idea we weren't in Heaven. He was awfully content in that fluff of white clouds. I don't think he has moved from that spot in two-thousand years.

I said to him,
"God bless you, Henry."
He smiled at me, patting the clouds next to him.
It was an invitation to lie down and enjoy myself.

I obeyed.
We were on our backs, side by side, looking at the sky. LaFelle replayed one of his memories. The aether morphed into a vibrant evening on Earth. I think a shooting star went by.

We talked about his imagination. I congratulated him for being so sharp, even after all these years. Most people had lost half their memories by now. Two-thousand years was a long time, it seemed.

"Got plenty of time," the old farmer said.

It's true. Unlike on Earth, we now have all the time we want.

LaFelle went on telling me about the night sky at his farm. He swore there was no way he could forget how beautiful it was.

I told him that I was jealous. I wished I had something beautiful to hold onto.

The farmer rolled his eyes at my comment, patting my shoulder.

"Son," he said, "keep thinking like that, and you'll never have anything beautiful at all."

I was embarrassed.

Somehow, even this far from Earth, I felt shame.

LaFelle was not the type of person to embarrass anyone. He did not think it was strange when people said stupid things. He knew we were all stupid anyway, and didn't see a point in hiding it.

Still, it would have been nice to get the approval of my savior. He found me in the smoking wreckage of a train.

***

Up on that patch of clouds, waiting for God to show up, I listened to how Henry found me.

The farmer said he was on his way home from buying chicken feed and gasoline. Halfway between town and his farm, a cloud of smoke was floating into the sky.

He followed it, taking his truck off road, into a dirt field. LaFelle said he always liked that field. It put a nice gap between him and civilization. Train tracks rested there, though he never saw the train go by.

"Not until you bellied up," he said, staring at the stars. "I had a feeling there was something to be found under all that smoke."

Henry went on, talking about how he drove for a while into the field. It was getting dark out, so he flashed his high beams. He couldn't believe they still worked.

Eventually he found the train.
It was in pieces, scattered across the field.

He searched the wreckage for hours, seeing only by his flashlight and the glow of so many fires. Parts of the train were still burning when he got there. According to Henry, he could have *"Hunkered down by a nice campfire, and cooked up some 'dogs."*

Apparently, after all that searching, Henry found three survivors.
One of them was awake.

***

"Which one?" I asked.
He was looking for a name, but couldn't find one.
"The big guy," he said.

He meant Bulgruf.
Somehow, we both survived the crash.

"Good thing the big man was awake," Henry said, "otherwise he'd have been in Heaven a lot sooner."

We were silent for a while. Henry's imagination was a good show. It was full of stars.
"I always thought you two were a good couple," he said.
"Yes, Bulgruf is a wonderful partner," I said.
He chuckled.
I knew he meant Flyes.

What he didn't know was that Flyes would have made a cute couple with anyone back on Earth. Even with another woman. Especially with another woman. I think now that I would love to see Flyes with another beautiful woman.

I thanked God, wherever he was, for my lack of a penis. No one wants an erection in front of Heaven.

Henry met Flyes, of course.
He carried her inside after driving us all the way to his farm house.
She was the third survivor. LaFelle discovered her hanging upside down by her seatbelt, bleeding from the nose.

12

I MENTIONED that I no longer have a penis.
It fell off on the way to Heaven.

A lot of things disappeared when I got here.
I no longer have the voices telling me to rape or murder people, or to jack off in a bathroom. I think the clouds are made of Dr. Dan's magic medicine. Maybe he is somewhere in the distance, prescribing it to God.

I would be flattered to have the same medicine as God. I wonder if He ever had voices.

If He did, they probably told Him to create a beautiful universe.
Then, they told Him to make only one planet with life.
Then, they told Him to make that life kill itself.

I think the magic medicine would have helped.
Everyone needs a cool towel on their brain.

***

One thing I still have is a hole in my stomach.
I got it when a part of the train shot through me.

LaFelle wonders how that didn't kill me. I told him that there was a guardian angel. Everybody had one. Somehow, two-hundred guardian angels were late for work that day.

***

Like most people up here, my memory is fading. However, I still remember waking up in the bed of Henry's truck.

I opened my eyes.

I was inside a garage, one I had never seen before. Three of the walls were made of wood planks. They were measured right, sanded, drenched in linseed oil. It was a beautiful garage. The main door was open, as if someone were ready to take the truck out for a ride. No one did that. The driver, unbeknownst to me, was in the farm house, making breakfast.

Hindsight tells me that I sat up, rubbed my eyes.

Somehow I was in a garage.

That was fine.

I didn't argue with the universe.

***

I looked down.

There was a bandage wrapped over my abdomen. Its fabric was caked in dry blood.

It didn't hurt at all.

Somehow I stumbled out. I limped around, looking for clues. There was not much in that place. A rack of tools against the wall, a desk with nothing on it but a dead lamp. Next to that, a pile of old road signs. I thought that was strange. It would make a cute, minor detail in my novel.

There was a storm outside too.

It was a gentle storm, the kind that whispers and sprinkles. It meant that something big was coming.

The truck was in the middle of the garage.

I looked in the front seat, saw Bulgruf.
He was asleep with his head against the dashboard.

***

I slapped the window.
Bulgruf jumped, hit his head on something.

After that, I don't remember much.
I think he took a nitroglycerin pill, cursed at me for a long time about being foolish.

At some point, Henry came through the garage door. He must have heard all the commotion.
He looked at us, smiling. The man seemed totally relaxed, didn't think anything was strange about this whole meeting.
Next, Henry told us breakfast was ready, and that it was time to *"Come and get it."*

We must have been relaxed too. We must not have thought it was very strange.
After all, we obeyed.
Bulgruf and I walked inside to get breakfast.

13

My HEART TELLS me I was rescued.

Hindsight tells me I was kidnapped.

LaFelle tells me it made no difference so long as you were having fun.

I think he's right about that.

What I know for sure is that when Bulgruf and I walked inside, there was breakfast ready. The farmer had a small kitchen. It looked dry, made of wood and stone. No art on the walls, no pets. It was warm, though. I think the oven was heated by burning wood. On the ceiling, there was a metal grate. Herbs and dry vegetables were hanging, ready to be plucked and crushed.

The table was made from wood planks, which looked identical to those in the garage.

On top were four rectangular cuts of burlap. Each displayed a bowl with silverware and a mug.

There was a song playing in the background. It came from an old turntable.

Henry was by the stove, stirring a cauldron with his wooden spoon.

He said,

"Business or pleasure?"

***

It was funnier when he said it.

I think that's because he was already content with his life, stirring a pot of what he would later call, *"Breakfast soup."* He didn't need the joke. The farmer was happy. Happy people could make jokes all day, funny or not, and you would smile.

"Both," I added, unsure of what I meant.

He invited us to sit down. We obeyed.

"How's that belly?" He asked me, adding a dash of spice to the cauldron.

"Can't feel a thing," I said.

"Well, that's on account of the *cloud paste.* "

"The what?"

"The cloud paste," Henry said. "It's made from a certain tree bark, honey, certain leaves. Don't ask for the special ingredient. I won't give it up."

"Cloud paste," I said. "What's it got to do with clouds?"

The farmer turned around with his cauldron of stew, bringing it to the table.

"Keeps your head in the clouds," he said. "You don't feel the slightest concerned right now, do you? That you're in a stranger's kitchen?"

He was right. I felt perfectly fine.

"And you," the farmer said, pointing to Bulgruf, "I reckon you feel just fine."

He nodded. We both felt suspiciously fine.

"Big dose for a big boy."

Bulgruf scanned his body, looking for where the paste could have been.

"Yep, you can thank that special ingredient," Henry said.

***

69

Back then, two-thousand years and six days ago, the farmer told us what happened to the train. We were all eating breakfast at the time. It was the most peaceful kidnapping in history. If I had been dosed with any more cloud paste, I might have wanted to do it over again.

"The name's LaFelle," he said, "Henry LaFelle."
That name echoed.
"LaFelle Farms?" I asked.
"Sure enough," he said, "I guess word does get around."
I told him I recognized the name from my childhood. I used to travel all over California with my nanny, Roselle. We loved farmers' markets back then.

Bulgruf spooned breakfast soup into his mouth. He seemed perfectly fine, listening to the two of us talk.

We were on farmland just outside San Francisco, California. LaFelle's property was two-hundred acres. With stew in our bellies, and our heads in the clouds, Henry went on talking about how the farm came to his family. Or rather, how they kidnapped it:

***

His ancestors were pioneers.

The original LaFelle was a tracker and survivalist from the Rocky Mountains. He went west, on account of there being tremendous wealth in the form of gold. The pioneer gathered a huge party of men and supplies, and set off.

Once they landed on the West Coast, LaFelle befriended local, native tribes. They were called *Indians*. Indians were uneducated barbarians who, God bless them, did not have any gold. They survived by growing corn, catching fish, hunting deer. They found sweet fruit hanging from trees and growing out of the soil. They even discovered that growing certain plants after corn season would replenish the nutrients for next year. They drank water directly from the sky.   One such Indian met a white pioneer and his friends while hunting. The pioneer, in order to express rapport, put a musket in the barbarian's hands, and a hat onto his head. The Indian, in order to express rapport, showed the man to his village. It was full of bronze-skinned barbarians who were so uneducated, they couldn't use the musket. It was alien technology to them. So, they all just admired it.

There was a feast, and the white explorer hugged the barbarians before he went home. Later that night, the pioneer returned to the village. He was white and educated, so he could easily remember things he had been shown. He arrived with fifty-three friends this time. They all had muskets. They knew how to use them.

They opened fire on the village for exactly five minutes and zero seconds.

Apparently, that was how long it took for every villager to be shot.

The pioneer looked over the body of his bronze-skinned friend, and took the hat. Apparently, the barbarian fell asleep wearing it. He died full of musket rounds.

The place was renamed *"LaFelle Plains"* in honor of the man who liberated it. The hero's name was sewn into his hat with yellow thread: *"LaFelle"*. The hat was passed down to his son, along with the story of how it won the war against the barbarians. Well, that son gave it to a son of his own, and so on. Eventually, in nineteen seventy-five, it was placed on a little boy's head.

The little boy would become a man, by and by.

He would learn to be a farmer.

***

Henry pointed to the coat rack on the wall. The old, pioneer's hat was hanging by a hook.

"It's right there, if you reckon I'm a liar."

I told him I believed him. Bulgruf nodded too, eating another bowl of soup.

"Well," Henry said, "I wish I were lying. Ain't no good come from people killing people. That's why I don't wear the hat. Bad karma sewn inside, right with my name. And *Mother* hates bad karma."

My soup was still too hot.

"Mother?" I asked, blowing on my spoon. I hadn't noticed any mothers around.

"Mother," he said, lighting a match over his stove. "She's all around us. You can thank Mother for that cloud paste. All its ingredients came from her. *We* came from her."

I thought that was beautiful. I was going to plagiarize that in a novel.

He put the lit match under a home-rolled cigarette.

"Excuse me," Bulgruf said, "what have you got there?" He motioned an invisible cigarette against his lips.

Henry smiled, extending the joint to his guest. It was full of illegal plants.

"No thanks," Bulgruf said.

The music stopped.

LaFelle walked over to the record player, flipped the vinyl, dropped the needle. Another song was going. It was grainy and full of charisma.

"Yep, she's all around," Henry said, picking up a newspaper he had by the sink. "And I reckon bad karma is on a rise these days. Mother is pretty pissed off."

He went on to tell us about himself.

Ten years prior, LaFelle had been the regional coordinator of Western Federal Meteorology.

I was shocked by that.

He sounded like he had not stepped off the farm in a hundred years.

But what he said was true.

Before retiring, he was paid over one-hundred thousand dollars a year. Western Federal Meteorology was a small division of the national government which kept track of serious weather patterns. He never talked about why he left. All Henry had to say about it was that he *"Knew people."* Apparently, the man had tremendous connections to the scientific world and to the United States' government.

All his *"people"* agreed that the world was ending in six days. Apparently, storms were coming sooner than the news warned. Much sooner. And they were ten times larger than the news said they were.

***

Looking back, I now realize why he used cloud paste to cover my wounds. I needed to be high for that kind of conversation.

It continued like this:

Henry said that the oceans were stuffed with trash and oil. The atmosphere was suffocating on pollutants. Apparently, Mother's immune system was no longer forgiving.

Those were LaFelle's exact words:

"No longer forgiving."

I thought that was beautiful.

That cloud paste was made with magic, I really believed. Its magic flushed through all my vessels.

It didn't even hurt when he described *how* the world would end.

"Huge hurricanes," he said, "bigger than you've ever seen. Bigger than anyone's ever heard of. Wind over three-hundred miles an hour."

I looked at Bulgruf.
His mouth was open.

"And," Henry said, "that ain't even what's going to kill us."
He poured some coffee onto his empty plate. The dark fluid spilled over, covering everything.
"Those storms will be torturing the oceans. I'm talking walls of water three miles high."
He motioned with his hand, swiping the air in front of him. It meant the world would be crushed by water in six days.

***

Henry slapped the newspaper onto the table in front of us.
"And," he said, "that's how it happened, boys." He was pointing to the article on the front page.
"That's how what happened?" I asked.
"That's how you broke down on the way here, in your big train."
I looked at the front page:

"Two-hundred Dead in Largest Act of Domestic Terrorism."

At the time, I forgot to thank God for my high. Without it, Bulgruf and I would both be dead from heart attacks. We had never gotten so much bad news in one day.

"Wow," I said, "what a shame." I sipped the coffee LaFelle made for us. It was flavored with hazelnuts. It was more powerful than the newspaper.
"And," Henry said, tapping the paper, "this is their last issue. It says so, right at the bottom."

I realized Henry was talking about the Western Sun. This paper was published by them, the largest news circulator in California.

And what Henry said was true.

In bold print, right on the front page, it told all its readers that this would be the last paper it ever printed.

The Western Sun, after all, would soon be destroyed, on account of the apocalypse.

14

HINDSIGHT REMINDS ME of my initial reaction:

"Great. Now who's going to hire me?"

At that point in my life, I was twenty-nine in human years. Historically, most humans who made it to twenty-nine were veterans of tragedy. They had been eaten by dinosaurs or died of the flu, or something.

I had been blessed with only two tragedies.

One of which, I was rescued from. My rescuer was a nice farmer who got me high and fed me breakfast.

So, I was a veteran of tragedy.

And then, after reading the newspaper, I almost shit my pants.

Good thing that cloud paste was in my system.

***

I looked at Bulgruf.

He was shaking his head, sipping coffee.

He did not realize it at the time, but this was the very catastrophe he'd been fighting his whole life. His scientific career was devoted to saving the world from natural disaster.

In its very last stand, the Western Sun reminded two men, full of breakfast and drugs, that they were failures.

"Listen," Henry said, rolling up the newspaper. "There's hope."

He said something about *arks*.
It was almost unbelievable, but I was high.
Arks were like spaceships, but made to float around in Earth's atmosphere. Henry said they could resist even the worst hurricanes and storms. When the water was calm, they could float on top.
I was relieved. It was a miracle.
LaFelle said the same thing. He called it *"Science's apology."*

Science, he argued, got us into this mess. It tempted us with convenient technology. That technology pissed off Mother with its wastefulness.

LaFelle said, "Convenience ain't no good when there's nothing to use it on."
In other words, convenience would die with planet Earth.

***

Still, I was thankful for the miracle of science. It dipped us over a fire, and pulled us right back up.

I forgot to thank God for science.

My mind was too busy drooling over the arks. Henry said they were hundreds of miles long. They would be able to carry millions of human beings. They had artificial ecosystems and energy renewal devices.
Suddenly, the apocalypse seemed very nice.
I was excited.

"Yes sir," LaFelle said, "you get down to San Francisco, all you have to do is prove you're an American citizen and voila. Welcome to Eden."

"That's it?" Bulgruf asked.

"That's it," Henry said. "And don't worry about no social security or ID. As long as you look American, you're in."

That was good enough for me.

I was ready to watch the world die from the seat of a spaceship.

**

I remember the old farmer talking about San Francisco, California.

The arks were waiting there to pick us up.

Human beings were there too, waiting to kill us.

In fact, they had tried to kill us already.

As I said before, the Global Church of the Almighty Creator had its own idea of salvation. It did not involve any spaceships. They thought a purge would do the trick.

**

"Says so here," LaFelle said, tapping the paper.

He was right.

The Western Sun had an article about the Church's ten-thousand disciples in San Francisco, California. Apparently, they had been getting increasingly ornery for months. They had blocked traffic, wrecked public property. A hobo was beaten to death in their plaza.

For some reason, the police never interrupted.

"It's Sullenous," Henry said, looking at Bulgruf and I. "The High Priest. He puts all the money into the governor's pocket. And the governor keeps the police away."

Bulgruf shook his head. He was still very high on cloud paste.

Henry said Sullenous wanted to destroy San Francisco, a city of sinners. The Church was proving to God that good people were still on Earth.

***

"Cat and mouse," LaFelle said. "Stay away from them, and you're golden."
I asked him if the government really wasn't going to do anything about it.

"About what?" he asked.
"About the riots, the terrorism." I thought it was a pretty obvious question.

Henry told me, joint between his lips, that the government no longer cared. It, and everything it governed, was going to be underwater in six days. Apparently, the government and their scientists knew all about the end of time. They decided to not break the news. In fact, they made sure the news said disaster was still postponed for another ten years. It was better that way. People were not known to stay calm under pressure.
"Yep," Henry said, "ain't no more government. Without saying a word, they up and left their offices. They're home, with their families. Don't make sense to fight no more. No more sense in trying to separate right from wrong. Hell," he said, lighting the end of another joint, "they're happier now than ever."
He extended the joint towards me. Its end was glowing red.
I took it, inhaled.
I supposed he was right.

The room smelled like San Francisco, California. It was full of THC and organic breakfast. The apocalypse was on its way, and we felt fine. We might have even gone out later for matching tattoos. They would say, *"Music is my religion,"* or *"coexist."*

Those were mature things to put on your body.

I smiled at that, dragging more smoke into my lungs.

The farmer rolled another joint, right there on the kitchen table.

Outside, rain pelted the roof, trickled down the windows.

LaFelle said that gentle rain was a sign of the storms. They were brewing. Apparently, Mother was starting to warn us about the end of time.

It was a nice thing for her to do.

The rain sounded like an army of butterflies, all with little drums.

15

SOMETHING I FORGOT to mention:

I met Arthur Sullenous, High Priest of the Global Church of the Almighty Creator.

He was lounging around God's front yard, just like everyone else.

We met by accident.

I had said goodbye to my friend and savior, Henry LaFelle. On my way to the Gates for another round of apologies, there was another old man.

It was the priest.

On Earth, I wanted to kill him.
Up here, I just wanted to say hello.

Like my penis, vengeance disappeared in the afterlife. Most of our urges disappeared.

Henry is still lying down, for example.

That's all he needs.

I think he'll stay there, even when Heaven opens up.

Anyway, I met the High Priest.

I knew it was him because he was holding hands with a hobo. The hobo looked about ninety, in human years. His face was covered in bruises, and there were no front teeth. His neck was broken, keeping his head slanted. The hobo had nothing to say.

I said hello to the famous Arthur Sullenous.
He said hello. He was smiling.
Apparently, Arthur didn't feel shame this far from Earth.

***

We sat together on the clouds.
If God were watching, he might have thought it was a picnic.
I can't remember exactly where we were, but I think Flyes was singing in the distance. Her four friends were at it too, their voices like golden flutes.

"You tried to kill me," I said. It wasn't spiteful. I thought it was an interesting thing to say. There are not a lot of provocative things up here, outside Heaven.
"Well," Arthur said, patting his hobo friend on the back. "Join the club."

He told me about how that poor man was beaten to death in a church plaza, two-thousand years ago.
"Now, we're best friends," Arthur said. The hobo was silent. His voice was broken during World War II. World War II was a bunch of monkey business from two-thousand and seventy-one years ago. It involved a lot of pollution and dead bodies that got shoved underground. Somehow, a flower was involved.

***

Arthur was very nice to talk to.
His vocabulary was well polished.

"How many people did you kill?" I asked, imagining I had a cup of coffee. People loved to drink coffee back on Mother.
"Two," he said, stroking the hobo's neck. Bones were sticking out.

"Including this poor guy?" I asked.

"No," the priest said, "not him. Not personally."

He went on about how his disciples killed thirty-thousand people in the span of seven days. They destroyed as much of San Francisco as they could.

"Sounds like a lot of monkey business," I said.

"We certainly acted like a bunch of chimps."

"But not you," I said. "Not personally."

"Correct," he said. "But I was rubbing my penis with cocaine."

16

THE FOLLOWING is a true account, according to Arthur Sullenous, the most famous man from planet Earth. He had a human body, stuffed with a human soul, just like me.

This is the story of how he went to the afterlife:

When he was eighteen in human years, Arthur was staring out the window in his dorm room. That room was in the most expensive college in the United States of America. It was the autumn of nineteen seventy-five. A snowstorm was falling from outer space. Somehow, snow came early that year.

Arthur was alone.
His father paid extra for a single dorm. It was supposed to give him *"More room for studying, friends could wait."* His father made well over one-hundred thousand dollars a year. He was the chief executive officer for the largest weapons manufacturer in America. He made sure that his son was prepared to become rich too.

Arthur had a cigarette in his lips, face close to the glass.
There were no stars that night. They were covered by dark clouds.
His room was dark too.
Arthur was deep in a daydream.
It whispered this, over and over:

"He will not make it back to Earth."

Arthur wanted that to be the last thing people said about him. In his daydream, the coroner stood by Arthur's dorm window. Supposedly, the boy fell from it, landing to his death.

But when police arrived, the window was closed. It wasn't even broken.

Arthur's body was nowhere.

In his daydream, the young man was sucked into a black hole. It stripped his atoms, one by one, through the window. Soon, there was nothing left.

The boy was prepared for that. So, by the window, the coroner would find a dying cigarette, and a letter that said,

"It's not your fault."

It was addressed to the people of Earth.
The next day, the newspaper would say this:

"Body of Local College Student Missing."

Finally, his tombstone would say this:

"Here lies Arthur A. Sullenous.
He never made one-hundred thousand dollars a year."

***

He went to a party that night.

It was Friday. Fridays were very persuasive. They convinced everyone that all their responsibilities disappeared. Somehow, they got sucked up by black holes.

Arthur needed a black hole more than anyone.
If he did not get one, he was going to kill himself.

He had a full bottle of painkillers for just such an occasion.

But that night, he didn't do it. And he didn't tell anyone about doing it.

Or maybe he did. No one knows.

The memory of that evening is drowned in alcohol and vomit. Nothing that follows is for sure.

Somehow the party was over. There might have been cops. Arthur might have run away, getting in the clear.

Somehow he made it to his dorm building. He might have landed on all fours, throwing up vodka and stomach acid.

The pay phone next to him was ringing.

He might have answered.

Somehow, his cousin was on the phone. She was crying. She said something about *"He left me"*. Something about cutting herself too deep, said she was sorry. Something about nine-one-one.

Arthur ran to his car.

***

I asked the priest what happened next.

His imagination put us in the front seat of an American muscle car. The ride had clean paint and nice leather seats. It was a gift for his eighteenth birthday.

The windshield was dissolving under so much snow.

In the speedometer, a red arrow pointed to ninety.

We swerved, crossing yellow lines.

Somewhere, we hydroplaned.

The priest's memory was getting darker.

Eventually, it was black.

***

LETTERS FROM A HOBO

"That's where it happened," Arthur said to me. "Muscle car had to be taken to the junkyard. Front end was destroyed. Never saw it again."

I asked about his cousin.

He told me she survived. Paramedics found her face-down in a puddle of her own blood.

"She had the nicest oriental rugs," Arthur said. "I think they came from her parents. Anyway, she bled all over them. Don't know whatever happened to her after that. Think she had a kid, was living somewhere in Colorado." He thought it was a shame. Arthur really loved his cousin. It was the daughter of his maternal uncle. That uncle and his wife both died from heroin when they were twenty-seven.

We talked about the other car, and if anyone survived.

It was a family in there. The mom went through the windshield. Dad broke his neck against the airbag. But their ten year old son survived.

He was found hanging upside down by his seat belt, bleeding from the nose.

"They were on their way home from some banquet," Henry said, looking at the aether clouds. "Back then, I wished I could have traded my dad's life for the people I killed."

We were then standing in his parent's mansion.

***

After the crash, Arthur Sullenous dropped out of college.

If he could, his father would have sent the boy to Hell.

Instead, silence was his father's weapon of choice. The last thing he said to his boy was, *"I should have pulled out."*

Arthur's mother had nothing to add. She sat quietly behind her husband.

He never saw his parents again.

FRANK DONATO

Worst of all, Arthur never saw a drop of his father's fortune.

***

By twenty-two in human years, the boy had joined the Global Church of the Almighty Creator. They offered him redemption, which he needed more than ever.

Here's how that happened:

Arthur had a done a good job escaping his life of luxury. He hated science and business, so dropping out made sense. Killing two human beings gave him an excuse to leave his studies.

His next idea was to kill himself.

At twenty-one years, three-hundred and sixty-four days old, Arthur Sullenous was standing on a bridge. Beneath him was a river.

For some reason, there were no police around to stop him.

A car pulled up.

Someone stepped out, talking slowly. He asked Arthur what was going on, if there was anything he could do to change the boy's mind.

Arthur said, *"Give me hope."* It was the first honest thing he'd said in years.

The man said he had hope.

He really did have it. In fact, there were a billion people who had it.

***

The next morning, Arthur was twenty-two, in human years. He woke up in a beautiful townhouse in San Francisco,

California. A man and his wife had cooked breakfast, and they all ate together. It was a Sunday, and they were going to church. Arthur declined.

The man, his savior, looked at him and said,
"You asked for hope. It's a car ride away."

***

Years went by.

That car ride had turned into hope, as promised.

Arthur quickly became the most popular person in the congregation. He was intelligent, and spoke with a polished vocabulary. His words sounded like they were made of silver.

Arthur went on missions all over the world, spreading the word of the Creator. Under his leadership, the Church became the biggest religion on Earth.

Anyone who knew about the Creator, knew about Sullenous.

That popularity turned into priesthood:

When the High Priest died, Arthur was elected to serve as the new head of the Church.

***

"But," Arthur said to me, "something didn't feel right."
"What?" I asked.
"I don't think I believed most of what I preached."
"Really?" I asked.

Arthur nodded. He told me about his recurring nightmare back on Earth. It waited for him in his sleep every night:

He'd be walking down a street. There were no lights.

Eventually Arthur would meet two people in the dream.

A woman without a face. It had been ripped off by glass.

A man with a broken neck.

They took Arthur by the hand, started walking slowly.

They were taking him down the street.

He saw a fire in the distance. There were people screaming in the fire.

They screamed something about nine-one-one.

Arthur always looked down, but his feet were gone.

The street was gone too.

When he looked back up, the fire was gone.

The people were gone.

He screamed.

But his voice was gone.

"Every night," he said. "I couldn't believe in a god who allowed for all that."

***

When the Creator failed him, Arthur found salvation at the bottom of a bottle. Apparently, salvation could be bought for eleven dollars, plus tax.

Salvation was not for women who were pregnant.

"Let them drink," he'd say to himself, swallowing a bottle of salvation. "Last thing we need is more fuckers running around."

In his priesthood, Arthur discovered that human beings were nothing but fuckers. We were self-replicating technology. Our purpose was to use up resources.

Many nights, Arthur would pass out in his personal chambers in the capital cathedral. It was in San Francisco, California.

Too much salvation did that to people.

It gave them delivery from evil.

"And these fuckers are evil," he would say, locked in his personal chambers. He would look out the stained-glass windows and say to planet Earth, "Sorry about all this."

Arthur was apologizing on behalf of mankind.

His brain was dunked in salvation.

"Planet Earth," he asked, "are you the Creator after all? Are you the one we've been looking for?"

Earth was silent.

"Well," Arthur said, "we did come from you. Made from the same stuff, you and I. And you're plenty older. Did you make us? Did you know we would be so chaotic?" He paused, swirling the bottle of salvation. "Did you want us to kill you?"

Arthur gulped another mouthful.

"I would want to die," he said, breath hot with salvation. "I would want to die if I were as old as you."

***

Sullenous told me that eleven dollar salvation melted parts of his brain, and his liver. He told me that salvation made him believe Earth was trying to kill itself.

Humanity was a gun to the head, two-hundred thousand years in the making.

Arthur wanted to be an obedient creation.

He wanted to fulfill Mother's wishes.

"I got the people fired up," he said. "Didn't give a damn about the afterlife. Earth was the Creator, as far as I could tell."

"Fired up?" I asked.

Arthur told me that, after his revelation, his sermons were more passionate than ever. He never ran out of things to talk about.

Not for a while.

"I was trying to keep my visions," he said, "so the drinking never stopped."

He tried his best.

But soon, even salvation failed him. The visions disappeared. The passion died.

"And I had no idea what to believe," Arthur said. "So you know what I did?"

"What?" I asked.

"I said, *fuck it.*"

***

He told his followers a lousy tale about the Creator seeking to destroy mankind, since it misbehaved so much. Next, Arthur urged his congregation to fight against sinners.

"It gave them hope," he said. "That's all they ever needed from me. That's all they needed from anyone. I had already killed two people," he said, looking me in the eyes. "I was not going to ruin the hope of a billion more."

Arthur shook his head.

"And they went for it. They did whatever I asked. That's how this guy got hurt," he said, patting the hobo's shoulder. "Everyone believed me."

I was quiet for some time.

We sat on a white fluff of aether clouds, a few miles from Heaven.

Arthur Sullenous eventually told me about the last sermon he ever delivered.

At the time, he was nearly dead from salvation.

He no longer believed in the Creator.

He no longer believed in anything.

***

Sullenous rubbed his eyes.

He had fallen asleep in his personal chambers.

He woke up on Sunday morning with church service only a few hours away.

There was eighty-proof salvation in his brain.

"Late for class," he said, fumbling with his white robe.

Arthur was trying to tie a belt around his waist. It was difficult with drunken, old hands. So he thought about skipping the belt, letting his robes fall off. Everyone would see his penis dangling. He might even masturbate.

The holy water was set, ready to go.

In his left shoe was the key to the church car. It was a remodeled hearse, one that was made shorter. The vehicle had a shiny coat of white paint, and was only used for very special occasions.

That's all Sullenous needed. He would be gone within the hour. But his people still needed that hope.

Arthur told me sunlight was blaring through stained-glass windows in his personal chambers.

It lit the whole room with colorful fire.

Back then, he thought about if the Earth moved any closer to the Sun.

We would be incinerated.

It would be beautiful.

***

I asked him what happened next.

He told me about the church service. Everyone in the congregation came forth and sipped holy water, like they always did.

"It was stimulants," Arthur said. "Tasted just like water, though."

So, in one afternoon, the High Priest drugged ten-thousand people. The holy water was spiked with a new breed of cocaine. It was a hundred times more powerful, and lasted for two weeks.

Then, the priest told everyone to prove their devotion.

"The Creator is watching," he said. "Vanquish those who oppose him."

Apparently, everyone obeyed.

"They broke out the front doors, into the streets," Arthur said. "Destroyed whatever they could."

It was true.

San Francisco was burned alive by the least sinful people in the world.

There was no government to stop them.

***

So, Arthur Sullenous was the last person in the cathedral. Everyone else went out to kill sinners.

The priest was wearing a two-foot ceremonial headpiece. It was made of white velvet and silver. It showed that he was an important human being, and that he never sinned.

His body was wrapped in white robes. The man's feet were dressed in broken sandals. It was tradition that all priests should don the official footwear of the Creator. When the Creator came back to Earth, he was supposed to be wearing broken sandals.

For the first time in years, Arthur spoke to his god.

"Anytime now," he said. "Feel free to show up anytime."

Arthur took off his sandals.

"You must love it," he said, "that my imagination has been married to you for so long."

He pulled a bottle of salvation from inside the altar. There were two ounces left. Seven and one-half ounces were swimming through the old man's body. It melted part of his brain, unleashing a thought which had been trapped:

"I suddenly have nothing to do for the rest of my life."

Outside, a storm had rolled over. Sunlight was gone.

Thunder popped a hole in the sky. Rain fell out, pouring all over San Francisco. The cathedral's roof was pelted by water. It sounded like an army of butterflies, all with little drums.

Arthur looked at the bowl of water next to him.

It was tradition that before sermon, each member drank from the same bowl of water, which was blessed by the High Priest himself. Apparently, Sullenous had blessed that bowl with long-lasting stimulants. And what did the most powerful man in the world say to his ten-thousand jittering lunatics?

"Destroy everything."

So it was. They had crushed through the chapel doors, smashed out sections of stained glass. It was unbelievable what the human brain could take seriously when its chemicals were upside down.

A ball of fire had been held over the heart of the West Coast, and Arthur A. Sullenous dropped it.

***

So, for the first time in his life, Arthur could say whatever he wanted. He had nothing to do any more, and was officially retiring.

"Go fuck yourself," Arthur said. It was his first expression as a free man. "As a matter of fact," he said, raising a middle finger to his invisible audience, "I'll show you how it's done."

The priest removed his headdress, kicked it off the stage. It clanked down the steps, bouncing through the aisle.

His robe slipped off next.

Underwear dropped.

He splashed his hand in the bowl of liquid cocaine and rubbed his penis.

17

I DID NOT have a lot to say.

The hobo didn't have much to say either.

I wonder if he knew he was in the afterlife. The poor guy had no idea who he was holding hands with. He wasn't even sure how he died in the first place. He ran into a wall of fists, as far as he could tell. Worst of all, no one up here knows his name. He is still homeless and disfigured.

I wonder if the poor guy knows how close he made it to Heaven.

The aether clouds turned gray again. They looked like cotton candy with no flavor.

We were back in God's front yard.

I asked Arthur what he did next.

He said he jizzed all over the altar. His penis was hard for three days in a row.

That holy water was good stuff.

Later on, he stumbled into the little, white hearse. Its paint was white with crushed diamonds. It showed how pure the Church was.

"Drove it all the way there," he said, staring at the distance.

"Where?" I asked.

"To see Henry LaFelle. I wanted to apologize for killing his parents."

***

Two-thousand years ago, that would have sounded very dramatic. I would have wanted to write it in my journal. Later, I would want people to read it and think about how creative I was.

Now, I just wanted to go to Heaven.

So I told Arthur that we should go find Henry together. The priest could finally apologize. He could take the farmer's hand and say, *"I'm sorry for destroying your family with my car,"* or, *"I'm sorry for driving like an idiot."*

But that never happened.

"Don't worry about it," Arthur said. "I've already delivered my atonement. We died together, Henry and I."

"Really?" I asked.

"Really," he said. "I'm sure Henry would love to tell you all about it."

That would happen, later on.

18

Anyway, I left the High Priest.
We shook hands, said it would be nice to meet again.

Back on Mother, I had no idea about Arthur's personal monkey business. I had no idea about Henry's parents. My soul was stuffed inside a human's body. I didn't know much.
Everyone had a body that didn't know much.

***

Back to Henry's kitchen.
A beautiful woman walked downstairs and sat next to me.

It was Flyes.

"Hey," I said.
I couldn't believe I said that. We survived terrorism together. She at least deserved *"Hello,"* or, *"I can't believe you're here."*
I went with *"Hey."*

That reminds me:
I had sex once on Earth. It was my twenty-first birthday. I met someone at a bar, bought her drinks. Somehow we stumbled inside an unlocked church at midnight, our brains full

of alcohol. The next morning, I woke up with my pants around my ankles, covered in vomit.

It was a Sunday.

So, beautiful women had an effect on me: they reminded me how incompetent my penis was. Men spent half their lives trying not to be a bundle of sticks. The other half was spent measuring their penises.

Of course, that's all I could think about when Flyes walked downstairs, into Henry's kitchen. She was wearing sweatpants and a hoodie.

I was wearing a penis that was exactly four and a half inches long.

The farmer's penis was almost eight inches long.

Bulgruf, if he could ever find his penis again, would discover that it was six and three-fourths of an inch long.

***

My brain was busy wondering what it might be like to *bone* her. That was another word for affection, back on Mother.

These days I wonder why boning disturbed me so much as a young man.

It was very important, on Mother, how many times a person got boned.

I never got boned. I wasn't a bundle of sticks.

Though, I was afraid of becoming one.

I think not having a penis helps with all that. No more chemicals in my brain. No more voices. Nothing to be embarrassed about.

I wonder if Arthur is glad his penis is gone.

It was hard for three days in a row.

***

Anyway, Flyes really did come downstairs to join us. I was high on THC and cloud paste. Seeing Flyes was a whole other kind of drug, I'm sure. She was alive, which I couldn't believe.

More importantly, she was still beautiful.

We talked for a while, listening to the butterflies and their drums.

I think Flyes had some THC. She certainly had cloud paste, too. It was one of the few things that stopped her from being such a bitch. I watched her eat breakfast. She had very little to say.

Soon, we were in the garage again, packing for our journey to San Francisco, California. The bed of the truck was loaded with gifts from Henry. There was food, waterproof matches, a few ponchos, and so on. Outside, rain came down hard.

Henry told me there was enough gas to get us to the city, but not enough to waste on detours. He said to sleep inside if we could.

Then, he put the keys in my hand.

"You're not coming?" I asked.

"No sir," he said. "Captain goes down with his ship."

That was that.

He would not be swayed. The farmer wanted to die with his two-hundred acres.

I don't blame him. It was the only family Henry had in forty years.

Also, he was expecting a visitor.

***

So I drove away with my new friends, all snug in the front seat. The heater was on. I even had a thermos of coffee in the cupholder.

Drugs really brought the three of us together.

We had a nice time with paste in our bloodstream.

Henry and his farm disappeared in the rearview mirror.

He was my savior. I would see him again in two-thousand years.

***

Rain poured over the West Coast wilderness. It was dissolving the backroads, flushing them away in streams.

"Sounds like butterflies on the roof," I said, listening to the rain.

"Butterflies," Bulgruf replied. His hot dog fingers were holding a photograph. I think it was a woman. She was wearing an old scarf.

He might have crushed her during sex.

"Who's that?" I asked.

"No one," he said, folding the picture in half, slipping it into his pocket.

Flyes was asleep again. Hindsight tells me she had a concussion.

"Did we get kidnapped?" I asked.

"I guess we did," he said.

I told Bulgruf I liked getting kidnapped.

He agreed.

In the cabin of that truck, Bulgruf lit the end of a joint. It was another going-away gift from Henry. It came with the words, *"Good luck out there."*

***

Bulgruf said, "I wish Henry had left me by the train."

"What do you mean?" I asked.

"Would have made dying a lot easier."

His head was leaning against the window. Outside, there were trees for miles.

"Henry's a good guy," I said. "God knows that was a disaster, getting your big ass in the truck."

I think Bulgruf smiled. It might have been the first time in forty years.

"God knows it," he said, breathing a cloud of smoke. "What else do you think God really knows?"

That question sounded very nice.

I wanted to write it in a bathroom.

"God, God, God," I said. "What does he know?" I drummed the steering wheel with my fingers, playing along with the butterflies. "No clue," I said, "but I could probably tell you what he hates."

"Me," Bulgruf said.

We laughed at that for a while, wondering if God hated us. The joint passed back and forth, getting smaller.

Flyes was asleep, head lying on rolled-up sweatpants.

I asked Bulgruf if science really knew anything.

He shrugged, looking out the window.

"It knows we are royally fucked."

***

We drove in silence for a while.

Only the rain spoke up. It was getting louder, pelting the metal roof.

Back on Mother, people were upset about the weather an awful lot. I don't know why. I always liked rain. I wish it rained outside Heaven sometimes.

Down there, the truck felt like a cocoon. Water spilled over us, but we were warm and dry. I was happy, driving closer and closer to the apocalypse. There was something about warm, rainy car rides. They dunked my soul in hot chocolate.

That made me wonder about the conductor.

I guess he died on the train.

I flicked the high beams on. Surprisingly, they still worked. That thing looked like it was the first truck ever invented. All its paint had rusted into the afterlife.

But the lights worked.

They worked so well, that I saw a man in the distance.

He was sloshing down the side of the road.

***

I drove up to him, rolling down the window.

"Hey bud," I said, shouting over the rain. "Where you headed?"

"To Hell!" He said.

It took me a few seconds to realize the man was naked.

No kidding.

He was old, skin hanging from his bones like dough. That dough was freckled with dark spots.

He wore nothing but loose underwear.

Underneath was a massive erection.

"Oh my God," I said, rolling up the window.

I stepped on the gas.

***

Bulgruf looked at me, shaking his head.

We never talked about that again.

***

A little red arrow glowed in the dashboard. It lingered around thirty.

I was a safe driver back on Mother.

One time I was pulled over for driving too safe.

The police officer told me to stop acting like a bundle of sticks.

So in Henry's truck, I drove slowly on purpose.

The apocalypse gave people like me more liberty than they ever needed.

I used that liberty to drive in peace.

In the distance, there was a white car parked on the side of the road.

I pulled up to it.

It was a beautiful, modified hearse. The headlights were still on, glowing like lanterns in the storm. The driver door was wide open. Inside, a song played from the radio.

"Anyone there?" Bulgruf asked me.

I told him there wasn't. It was true. The car was stuck in mud, engine still running. Exhaust smoked from the tailpipe. But there was no one inside.

I supposed it's where that naked, old man came from. He must have given up.

"Nice car," I said, driving away.

19

THAT NIGHT, I parked the truck on a cliff.

It was the edge of the United States of America. It fell one-hundred feet, into the Pacific Ocean.

I knew about that place from my childhood, when Roselle and I took trips across California. We would stop there with a picnic blanket and watch the horizon. I don't know what we talked about, or if we talked at all. She was eighteen, in human years. Somehow, we had common ground.

I imagined leaping off that cliff.

If I did, and I kept swimming, I would end up in a hurricane. It was somewhere out there, brewing in the Pacific Ocean.

Mother said so.

She was warning us with all that rain. It sprinkled the metal roof of our truck, spilling down the windows. I liked it. We were in a cocoon. For as bad as it was, the end of time sounded peaceful.

I clicked off the lights, turned off the engine.

At some point, Flyes woke up. She asked where we were. I told her the edge of America.

She told me to relax, that I seemed very on edge.
I smiled, wishing I had thought of that.

***

We talked about being kidnapped.
Said Henry was the nicest kidnapper in history.

She told me, "Maybe you can write about that in your journal."
I paused, looking at her.
My penis was filled with the idea that she recognized me. I was grateful for the darkness of the front seat.
"Didn't know I had so many fans," I said.
Flyes was stripping off her hoodie, revealing a camisole beneath.

"What else you got in that journal?" She asked.
"Oh, just some monkey business," I told her.

***

It was full of bad poems, things I plagiarized from all over the place. I even had a drawing of Flyes' vagina.
Imagine that.
Back on Mother, I had been inspired to draw vaginas.
And I gave it a shot, God knows. I put a lot of detail into her vagina.
It still turned out hideous.
Maybe it's a good thing that journal got lost forever.

***

There was a novel in there too. It would never be finished, much less published.
I had also written a story about a man who crushed women during sex. Another story was about a woman who hid french fries in her hair.

It was my brain between two book covers. It was horrifying. I would have shot myself in the face if Flyes ever looked inside.

I could do it.
It ran in the family.

***

I did mention the novel, however.
Told her about how I had wanted to publish a book, but was worried there might not be a printing press on the ark.
Flyes smiled at that.

So we went on about books.
I said that true stories were the best, and the easiest to take seriously. Flyes said she didn't read at all. Apparently, there was nothing provocative left in the world.
"Nothing left?" I asked. "Nothing at all?"
"Nothing," she said.
"So there's nothing I can write that would impress you?"
"Nope."
"Well," I said, "guess I'll have to find another way."

I think she smiled again.

***

Flyes told me to meet her ten years ago. That was when she could read all day, and might have agreed about the beauty of words. Back then, she even had a favorite book.

It was about a hobo.
He was losing his eyesight, and his mind. He lived in a collection of old boxes, in between two dumpsters. Apparently, the business that used those dumpsters was having construction done on its buildings. The hobo did not know

about this—companies were slow to give out memos to homeless men.

Anyway, he was feeling his way back to the old boxes. He wandered into a hard-hat zone. Construction had been going fast, and had reached the tenth story.

A loose two-by-four slipped from all the way up there. It busted through the man's skull.

He survived.

The project manager found him breathing.

Paramedics took him to shock trauma, where he was found to be in a coma. It was said that he would never emerge from that sleep.

But there was something the doctors didn't know.

His brain had been hit in just the right way: the man was stuck in a permanent dream.

It was true.

Wherever his brain landed first, that's where he would stay.

Here is where his dream landed:

He was a poor again.

He had no recollection of the dumpsters or the two-by-four. In his dream, there were trees for miles. The vibrancy of all colors had been amplified, as if God turned up a dial somewhere.

He was standing in a little patch of strawberries. There was a small, wooden house behind him, and a woman standing in the doorway. Her hair fell down in vibrant locks, and she never needed make up. She said, with a smile,

"Well, aren't you going to start picking?"

So he did. He picked the strawberries. He also discovered a chicken coop. He went and fed the chickens, gathered up all their eggs. The man stayed outside all day, raking in food and crops, taking care of the farm, staring at the trees.

Inside the wooden house, he was greeted by two little children who hugged his legs. His wife was there too.

She kissed him.

Later that night, they made love.

Years went by.

All of them were more beautiful than the last. Soon, the children moved away. He and his wife had somehow never aged. They didn't question it. Peace was peace. The universe had always been a strange place. So the two just went on loving.

In the book, time went faster in the man's dream.

After forty-eight hours at the hospital, he was unplugged from life support.

There was no one to notify, and nobody to object.

The doctor and nurse looked at him and said, as sadly as they could, *"What a shame."*

In his dream, the man had lived for years in the little wooden house in the big, deep woods. He made love to his woman every night.

On his last night, while she was in his arms, the man looked at her.

"I love you," he said.

"I love you, too," she said back.

And then, as peacefully it could, the world closed his eyes.

20

So, I am alone up here.

I've been wandering pretty far from the Gates. There are rumors about God walking around outside, talking to people.

We'll meet at some point, I suppose.

Right now, I am thinking about that night in the truck.

Flyes fell asleep on my shoulder. I don't blame her. There was nowhere else to lie down. And there wasn't much more to talk about. She got tired fast, couldn't keep her eyes open.

Back then, we were sleeping in the Milky Way galaxy. It was going two-million miles an hour through space.

I wonder whatever happened to the Milky Way, and where it went. Some scientists back on Mother thought it might crash into another galaxy.

I wonder if that cliff is still there.

Of course, my memory is dying fast.

Most of what I say might be untrue.

But like most humans, I claim to have tried.

I have been dead for much longer than I was alive. It makes sense that my memory is fading. Every day, it gets harder to think about the old times.

I'm trying to imagine Flyes on my shoulder again.

In that truck, going two-million miles an hour through the universe, my human body was in love.

So, I guess I've spent more time out of love than in it.

***

Sometimes the aether clouds don't work. Rather, my mind isn't strong enough. It has a hard time fitting the pieces back together, making sense of everything.

Right now, it won't show me what it looked like to be in love. Won't show me Flyes.

Maybe that's good.

When I close my eyes up here, everything goes black.

That hasn't changed since Earth. I'm grateful for the privacy that comes with closing my eyes. These days, I always thank God for privacy.

Sometimes, when my mind is dark and private, I hear something. I can't tell what it is, but I like it. I wish I heard it more often. In the distance, It'll sound something like butterflies.

And then, when I listen closely,
It's gone.

21

T<small>HAT NIGHT ON THE CLIFF</small> was covered in magic.
The morning after was covered in deep fog.

I woke up slowly in the front seat of Henry's truck. The rain had already been awake for hours, trickling softly down the glass.

I looked over.
Bulgruf was gone.
Flyes was still there, and still asleep. At the time, I thought it was adorable. She was curled up, head resting on her rolled-up sweatpants.

Hindsight tells me that, every minute, she was falling closer towards a coma.

There was a campfire outside, right on the edge of the cliff. Bulgruf was stoking it with a branch.

"The last pioneers," I said to myself, looking out the windshield. I saw embers glowing in the fog. Sparks popped, floating away.
It was nice to be a pioneer. My daydream said that Bulgruf and I met in the woods. We decided to stick together. The West Coast was dangerous, after all. Along the way, we found an injured woman. She was hurt by a musket round.

Apparently, her village was attacked by another pioneer and his fifty-three men.

I smiled at my daydream, opening the driver door.

***

"How's the girl?" Bulgruf asked. He was crouched by the fire, stirring a pot of soup.

"Asleep," I said. "Is that all for you?"

He smiled, tapping his spoon against the pot. He was playing along with the rain.

We talked about campfires, and how to cook on them. Apparently, he'd been doing it for forty-one years.

"Back when I started out," Bulgruf said, "it's all I had."

"Started out where?" I asked.

"Research," he said. "Environmental studies, down in the Andes Mountains. Spent most of my time outside the lab, as a matter of fact. First thing they taught me was the last thing I expected to learn."

I asked him what that was.

"How to stay alive. Make a fire, cook with it. I still have all those recipes," he said, tapping his skull. Bulgruf always remembered the things he'd been shown.

"People don't know it," he said, "but there's always something to eat out here. Believe me, you'd be hard-pressed to find something I wouldn't eat."

Bulgruf ladled soup into a bowl, handed it to me.

It came with a story about how he almost died in the mountains.

"Really?" I asked.

"Really," he said.

Apparently, it was him and one other researcher. They were both twenty-six, in human years, and on the edge of a cliff.

"We were on the edge when it collapsed beneath us. The other guy held onto my leg, dangling over a thousand foot drop," Bulgruf said. "Helicopter was out for hours, looking for the two fools battling with gravity." He blew on his soup, tasting it. "Somehow I held on."

Bulgruf said he came close to apologizing.

"I almost told the other guy how sorry I was," he said.

"Sorry for what?" I asked.

Bulgruf told me he was about to let go.

***

Then he asked about me, if I ever let go of anything.

I told him I hadn't.

"However," I said, "I was stuck in the mountains for a few years." I told him about my apartment in Denver, Colorado. For some reason, I had no good stories. I think I was too young to have stories. Sitting next to Bulgruf, I realized that life had happened around me, and never found its way in.

Now that I'm two-thousand and twenty-nine years old, I still have very little to talk about.

***

That morning on the cliff was a photographer's dream. Two men, sitting by a campfire on the edge of the world. Separated by a generation, brought together by the apocalypse. Behind them, and old pick-up truck was shrouded in fog.

If my life ever becomes a novel, that should be the front cover. Inside, there will be stories from Bulgruf. I'll write as if I had experienced them myself.

The title would say something apocalyptic, something sad and beautiful.

It would be everyone's favorite novel, even if they didn't read.

***

Bulgruf taught me how to make coffee on the fire, and which foods to find in the wilderness. He showed me how to keep the flames going even in the rain. It required a tarp. There was one tied above the fire, just high enough so it wouldn't burn. We sat underneath, feeling like the last pioneers.

I asked if he'd ever seen someone die in the Andes Mountains. He said he hadn't, not in the Andes. Not even in the jungle, or desert, or ocean. He'd been to places all over the planet, each with its own flavor of danger. But like me, the only time he saw death was close to home.

"One time I drove by a car accident," he said, "on my way to the airport." Bulgruf was prodding his soup with a spoon. "Happened forty-one years ago. I was stopped at a gas station with one pump. There was someone on it, but he unplugged the nozzle, gave it to me. Said his tank was already full, and that I might as well not waste the gas."

"It was a nice car," Bulgruf said. "Dark blue with no scratches. I thanked the man, watched his car drive back onto the road. He was older than me. Had a family in the car with him. It was his wife and their one son.

"Anyway," Bulgruf said, "I filled up, got back on the road. Drove for a while, until I saw that dark blue car again. It was upside down."

He said it was the autumn of nineteen seventy-five, and snow came early that year.

Two cars slid on that snow, crashed.

"I stopped next to it," he said, "there was a woman face-down in the street, covered in glass. I knew she was dead, must have crashed through the windshield. That nice gentleman was dead too, the one who gave me the gas. His eyes were still open, neck broken to the side."

Bulgruf paused, staring out at the edge of the world.

"There were two boys, matter of fact. First one must have been in college. He was the other driver, still in the front seat of an American muscle car, passed out on the wheel. Poor kid didn't have a hair on his face. I dragged him through the snow, into my passenger seat."

"The other boy, the son, must have been no older than ten or twelve. Found him in the back of that dark, blue beauty. He was upside down, hanging from his seat belt."

***

Bulgruf told me the two boys were still alive. He dropped them off at the first emergency room he could find.

He told the nurse to send paramedics, because there were still two bodies on the road.

"And then I left," he said. "Got on the plane, fell asleep."

We sat in silence for a while.

Wind blew up from the ocean, whispering our fire to death. It disappeared in smoke.

"Well," Bulgruf said, "guess it's time to get going."

22

I DO OWE an awful lot to the Global Church of the Almighty Creator.

Before the train exploded, I had no friends.

Thanks to the believers of San Francisco, I finally did.

The afterlife would be pretty boring without them.

And I owe something to Henry LaFelle's truck. It also helped me make a friend. His name was Habir Ashmood. In America, he was called a terrorist and a towel head.

I call him my friend.

He will be discussed, by and by.

***

So I thank the Church.

And I thank Henry's truck, too. If it were up here, I would sit in the front seat and pretend to drive it. I would imagine some rain, and a thermos of coffee.

It would be just like the old days.

In the old days, we left that truck on the cliff.

***

I lost the keys.

Hindsight is telling me nothing about where they are.

I had to wake up Flyes to help us look.

We spent two hours searching. I went through the car, under the seats. It wasn't there, or on the ground, or in the woods.

I thought a joke would help. I said a black hole took them in the middle of the night.

Bulgruf and Flyes told me to *"Jump off the cliff, the keys might be down there."*

I almost did that. In the moment, I hated myself, and everyone.

And I almost said that Bulgruf should come with me, *"Maybe he could finally let go."*

I wanted to tell Flyes to stay on the cliff, I wouldn't want her to cut her feet on the sharp rocks.

What I really wanted was to die.

I needed another asteroid.

But instead, I swallowed some magic medicine.

It was my last pill.

***

So the truck stayed there until it was dead.

It's somewhere in the Milky Way, going two-million miles an hour. The Milky Way is mostly dead, too. The rest of it, like I said, is lifeless.

And the three of us almost died as well.

We walked for two hours to reach the highway. Flyes' brain was bruised, Bulgruf's heart was thick with plaques. I was out of breath all the time. My abdomen felt fine, though. That cloud paste really worked.

Still, we would not be safe forever.

Rain drowned the West Coast. Clouds were morphing into dark, twisted shapes. It looked as if the sky was growing tentacles and crawling through the atmosphere.

It was Mother's immune system.
It was getting ready to kill us.

23

I'LL NEVER FORGET how terrible the traffic used to be in San Francisco. It's where I learned how to curse, when I was stuck on the highway with Roselle. It's where I wrecked my first car. I merged into a woman's sedan. We were both going two-million miles an hour through space.

Looking back, the storm did a good thing for that highway. It was almost completely empty.

When I try to imagine it now, I see a river flowing down the northbound lane, into the city. It carried a road sign that had broken off somewhere. It floated by, telling us to *"Yield."*

And I see the southbound lane. It was full of empty cars that had been escaping the city. I guess nobody wanted to go to church that day.

What else do I see?

Rain for miles.

Dark, twisted clouds.

I also see a man crawling on all fours.

***

That man was the terrorist.

He had brown skin and a stubble of thick, peppery hair. His name was Habir Ashmood, the towel head.

In the history of the universe, we met twice.

Once on Earth, once outside Heaven.

Habir looked like he died in his sixties. Back then, when I saw him crawling down the highway, I didn't ask how old he was.

But, outside God's kingdom, Habir Ashmood looked sixty. He wasn't wearing a towel, or a homemade explosive device. He was wearing a cord of barbed wire, tight around his neck.

"Habir," I said, hugging him. "You look as good as the day we met."

He smiled at me, took my hand.

That's what men did in his country, when they were going on long walks together.

We wandered for a while, holding hands.

Habir told me stories about the people he'd seen outside Heaven. He'd found his mother, who was old and beautiful. She died with a lump of cancer in her chest.

Near the Gates was the warlord who attacked Habir's village, and who shot his father to death. Habir even met his father. His chest had five holes in it. He was hand in hand with the warlord.

"Yes, and they both feel wonderful," Habir said.

"That's great news," I said. "God bless them."

He thought that was a nice thing to say.

He thought everything was nice.

So long as you did not call him a terrorist, he thought you were a genuine person.

So long as you did not hang him from a streetlight with a cord of barbed wire, Habir would take your hand, and walk with you for miles.

Even if you did hurt him, Habir would forgive you.

He forgave everyone for everything.

I wish Habir was God.

***

So that's all it took to make good friends on Mother. You had to look at a person, and be nice.

I could have done that. I never called Habir a terrorist. I certainly never choked him with barbed wire.

It was unfortunate that we met right before the end of the world.

Things were different in the clouds, when time didn't exist. Old friends counted for nothing when everyone lived forever. But, I still held his hand. Habir told me about his life on Earth. We walked, his imagination lighting the clouds on fire.

24

THE FOLLOWING is a mostly true account from the only terrorist I ever knew, Habir Ashmood. He was an honorary towel head.

This is how we met:

Habir's earliest memory was of his cat getting eaten alive.

The cat's name was Bulah.

Two-thousand and forty-five years ago, a warlord attacked Habir's village in Afghanistan. He sent famished dogs into each house, cleaning out survivors.

The dogs ripped Bulah in half.

***

That's what Habir was thinking about outside the gas station where he worked.

He was a robot, like everyone else.

He was full of wires and tubes and electricity.

Habir was programmed to say certain things, just like everyone else. This was all that was expected of him: *"Yes sir,"* or *"yes ma'am."*

He was sitting on the curb, wearing his uniform. It was a collared shirt. It said *Western Petroleum*, in big, green letters.

Western Petroleum made money by selling refined gallons of planet Earth.

Under those letters was a plastic name tag.

It said, *"Javeer."*

He never told his employers about the mistake.
No one used his name tag anyway.
His weekly checks were addressed to *"Javeer Assmoo"*.
No one cared.

Habir was twenty-two in human years. He had been in the United States for eight months, with his widowed mother. Her name was Pashmari. They shared an apartment together in a college-town suburb. It was across the street from the gas station.

The apartment building was entirely concrete. It certainly could have used drywall, or some kind of carpet. Habir imagined that all the workers gave up one day, quit their jobs. They must have gotten tired of concrete.

"Join the club," Habir said, blowing more smoke.

***

It was the autumn of nineteen seventy-five, and snow was coming early.

Habir held a cigarette close to his lips, watching his own breath. Smoke floated in gray, cursive letters, writing something in the sky.

Habir looked for words.

"Guess not," he said. "Maybe another language."

He was on the curb right outside the front doors.

Inside, he served as a robot cashier for Western Petroleum. Outside, the place was covered in posters. They promised winning lottery tickets and cheap gasoline. It was so dark out, the station's bubble of light was all a traveler would see on his way through town. If he stopped for cheap fuel or to win a million dollars, the traveler would find a terrorist on the curb out front.

His name tag was never used.
His real name was never used.

Pashmari was the only person in America who knew Habir's name. Unfortunately, she had nothing to say to him. His mother had nothing to say to anyone. She slept all day on a brain full of nicotine and alcohol. She had one hobby in the world: making parchment paper. She was good at it. It was something her husband taught her, many years before Pashmari moved to America. That was many years before her husband was popped open with bullets.

Habir told me about the parchment process. It involved a special paper, and a curing solution. His mother never passed down the secret ingredient in that solution. She really never spoke at all.

Another thing about Pashmari: she gave all her parchment away for free.
She sent it to a young, lovely artist in the basement of the apartment building. That artist was twenty-five in human years, and did housework for Pashmari while her son was away. The artist wrote beautiful poems on the parchment. She had millions of stories she wanted to tell through her words and paintings.
Another thing about the artist: she gave all her poems away for free.

***

Habir told me that he also had friends in the United States. He had friends before he ever met me.
They were hobos.
They lived around the college town, sleeping where they could. Habir had two dumpsters behind the station. He only

used one. The other he kept clean and untouched, so his hobo friends could sleep there at night. In the morning, Habir slipped a dollar from his own wallet into the cash register. Then, he would walk outside with cups of coffee for each hobo.

Habir lit another cigarette, watching the traffic lights go from green, to yellow, to red. They did that all night without any cars going by. Apparently, no one wanted cheap gas or to win the lottery.

Habir blew an alphabet of smoky curls into the sky, watching them disappear.

Across the street, there was a cat.

25

"Really?" I asked. "A real cat?"
"Really," Habir said. Apparently, it crossed the street.
"I asked if he was a good cat, then held out my hand."
Somehow, Habir knew the right words.
The cat approached him.

I saw all of this in the aether clouds.
There was a cat walking towards us. It had rough patches of white fur. There were scars all over its face.

"Then he licked my fingers," Habir said. "I still remember how scratchy his tongue was."

I felt it too, when Habir said that. For a moment, I thought something was licking my fingers.

I asked him what happened next.

"Well," Habir said, "I started calling him Bulah. I told him I was sorry he came back as another cat. I was sorry he kept getting hurt."

His memory went on and on, projecting into the clouds. I heard the cat purr. It rubbed its head on the terrorist's shoe.
Habir thought Bulah was telling him something: *"Don't apologize,"* Bulah said, *"it's not so bad being a cat."*

***

"I miss him," Habir said.

I asked what happened to Bulah.

He told me a car drove up to the station, scared the little cat away.

"I never saw him again."

In the aether clouds, we saw a dark blue car. It was beautiful, with no scratches.

Habir took the driver's money, went inside, put it in the register. I saw the driver pump his gas.

Then, another car drove up. A young man stepped out. The first driver gave his gas nozzle to young man.

***

From inside, Habir watched the blue car drive away. He saw a tall, handsome student pumping gas. He looked nervous, pacing back and forth, looking over his shoulder.

Habir was the most sympathetic human on Earth. From behind glass and posters, the brown-skinned terrorist said a little prayer for the man outside.

"There's a dog out there for everyone," he said to Bulah, who was gone. "Poor guy out there has some demons chasing him."

Habir was doodling in his sketch pad.

That was the man's only hobby: Doodling. He made fantastic little works of art in his book, adding to it every night.

Unlike my journal, his was full of real honesty.

Habir was a genius, trapped in a towel head's body, trapped in America.

In his book was a drawing of God.

It showed what was on the other side of the observable universe. It showed Habir from other dimensions, and in different time periods. It had a picture of two goldfish fighting each other for the ceramic castle at the bottom of a bowl. On another page, it showed those same goldfish working together to find a way out.

The towel head drew without thinking, letting the pen speak for itself.

That night was a picture of famished dogs, ripping a kitten to pieces.

"Bulah, Bulah, Bulah," he said. "There's a dog out there for everyone."

26

HABIR TOLD ME about the day San Francisco was destroyed. He was still working at Western Petroleum. It was the same one from nineteen seventy-five. There were more pumps, but they still sold winning lottery tickets. Across the street, his apartment building was still there. The place had undergone major renovations since Habir was young: it now had carpet.

So he lived in a carpeted home, all by himself.

"Mother died in nineteen eighty-two," he said, "a lump in her chest."

"I'm sorry," I told him.

He smiled.

I think that meant, *"It's not so bad, being dead."*

***

Habir left the city when he saw crowds forming.

"I knew they were trouble," he said. "The city behind them was on fire. I could see it from my bedroom window. Smoke everywhere. People running."

He shook his head.

The terrorist put on his coat, boots, and walked out the door. He didn't have a car. In forty years, the towel head never once applied for a driver's license.

Then, in two-thousand and sixteen, he walked again, until he got to the highway.

"No one stopped you?" I asked.

"Nope. I left just in time."

"Where were you going?"

He said he had no idea.

Habir told me that when he reached the ramp onto the southbound lane, he looked back.

He could still see the gas station.

It was on fire.

"They got to it," Habir said. "I heard screaming, too, from where I was standing."

I asked what that was all about.

Habir supposed it was the men who lived in the dumpsters.

Apparently, the disciples found three hobos rubbing each other's penises back there. They were dragged out, tied in barbed wire, doused in gasoline.

"And I guess someone dropped a match," Habir said.

***

The last employee of Western Petroleum took a walk down the highway. He splashed through the southbound lane, sliding between cars.

I saw everything in the aether clouds. Habir had a fabulous memory.

"And they were all empty," he said, pointing to the cars. "Everyone got out and left. We had so many things to run away from. Cars weren't fast enough."

I smiled at that.

I forgot I was holding hands with a terrorist.

131

We continued down the highway.

The clouds twisted in dark tentacles, drenching us with rain.

"Wildest thing I ever saw," Habir said, pointing at the sky. From there, he pointed to himself: a poor, old terrorist hunched over in the rain.

"That's when it happened," he said.

I watched as Habir bent over, threw up all over himself.

"I folded in half, started gagging," he said. "My stomach was full of fire."

"Really?" I asked.

Habir nodded.

He said it was acid reflux.

Habir had never been to a doctor. That day, while he drooled stomach acid, his lower esophagus was blooming with cancer. It had been growing more and more deranged every day for the past ten years.

"I fell over, it was so bad. That's when you found me."

It was then that I saw myself in Habir's memory.

I was standing there, emerging from the woods on the side of the highway. Next to me was a three-hundred pound man, and a prostitute.

Habir said he was praying when I found him.

"What did you pray for?" I asked.

He told God he'd like to be a cat, next time around.

***

Outside Heaven, the two of us watched history.

I saw it all, suddenly remembering it myself.

We helped Habir to his feet.

One arm over Bulgruf's shoulder, the other around mine. We waddled back to the city, sloshing through a mile of fallen rain. Then, we told him everything was ok, the arks were coming.

27

"Sorry," I said. I apologized for leading him to an earlier death.

That really happened.

I brought him back to the city, told him it was ok.

Then, he was murdered.

Habir said not to apologize. Apparently, there was a dog out there for everyone. They would find us all, eventually.

"These days, I thank my dog," he said. "It forced me to leave the city for once, even if it was just for one mile."

I patted him on the shoulder.

"God bless you, Javeer Assmoo."

***

So I said goodbye to my brown-skinned friend, gave him a hug. He was leaving to go spend time with his mother. Even this close to Heaven, she was insecure and lonely.

Later, I thought more about the time we found Habir, drooling on the highway.

I was glad he remembered everything. It sparked my mind a bit. Suddenly, I saw more.

We carried that poor, cancerous immigrant as far as we could. Eventually, he could walk again, and we made it back to the city. In fact, we walked right back up the southbound ramp. In the distance, I saw what was left of Western Petroleum. It was floating away into the atmosphere. Rain hissed against its burning carcass. There was smoke, and so on.

Back then, it took me a moment to realize where I was: We had made it to San Francisco, California.

My writing job was down the block. It was under a pile of burning rubble.

That much was true.

I met the chief editor outside Heaven.

He told me the disciples locked the doors from the outside, broke the windows. They tossed in Molotov cocktails. The first floor burnt to death, collapsing the rest of the building.

There were three-hundred employees inside.

***

I have to admit one thing.

The believers were very artistic. Their brains were drooling with cocaine and creativity.

They found interesting ways to get rid of sinners.

There was a wonderful little coffee house across the street from the cathedral. It had not been there when I lived in California. Back then, it was a shack. It was in the middle of an abandoned city block. The buildings had been dead from a storm years prior.

Then, a man named Spyros Marque bought the entire block.

Like me, Marque's father died early. His father's death became a check worth fifty-thousand dollars. Spyros used that money to acquire the dead buildings. He cleaned them up nice, but left them empty. He wanted people to make something good out of them.

So, the penniless Mr. Marque sold each unit to promising entrepreneurs for one dollar a piece. That was all it took. They each paid a single dollar for a slice of the property, so long as they promised to bring the place back from the dead.

And so it was.

One unit was reincarnated as a bakery. A married couple bought it, rebuilt it, decorated it. They became so popular, that every wedding in San Francisco needed one of their cakes. One time, they even made a cake for the first gay marriage in the neighborhood.

Another unit was reborn as a vintage clothing boutique.

Every unit got sold to someone who loved safe, beautiful cities, and had a good idea for a small business.

In the center of the block, Spyros fixed up the smallest building all by himself. He left the original, concrete floors, and put warm rugs on top. The walls were covered in exposed brick. Against those walls were leather seats and loyal customers.

Exotic coffee was brewed there every day. Each cup was a dollar a piece.

Spyros told me all this.

On my way back from seeing Habir, I met a stranger covered in ashes.

We decided to talk, since there was nothing else to do.

He said his name was Spyros, and that his memories were breaking into pieces.

It was a disclaimer: I could not trust anything he said.

So he went on telling me about the death of his coffee shop.

The disciples were fresh spiked on cocaine. Spyros saw them bust out of the chapel doors.

"I shut the storm sliders," he said. Storm sliders were retractable metal walls behind his shop windows. "Bolted the front door."

Then, he waited.

"Waited for them to crack our little shell open," he said.
"Did they?" I asked.
He said they did. But, his shop was the last to go.

The rest of the block was killed first.
They didn't have storm sliders.

***

The bakery owners were dragged into the street.
They were flattened with kicks and punches. Rain poured from the sky, washing their blood away. Somehow, they were still breathing.
A broken pool cue was duct-taped to the wife's hands.
Her husband was pressed face-down into the street.
His pants and underwear were ripped off.

"Let them eat their fucking cake," a disciple said, his friends watching.
He punched the woman. She buckled, knees splashed into the street.
The disciple grabbed her hands.

Together, they drove the pole through her husband's anus.

***

"Then the boutique," Spyros said. His face was dark with soot. "Nice gal," he said of the owner. "Trendy outfits. Great business woman. The day of the attacks, she had a cute chalkboard sign out front."
The sign said: *"Free spirits only."*
The believers smashed in her windows, pulled her out through broken glass. Her hands and feet were tied, mouth closed with duct tape.
"Time to free that spirit of yours," Someone said, knife in hand. Disciples made a circle around the woman. Rain poured

from the sky. It hissed against fire and hot bricks. Smoke and steam belched from the flaming ruins.

The disciple rubbed his knife through her scalp, peeling it all the way back.

***

I had nothing to say.

We were sitting down, looking at the Pearly Gates. They went on forever, making slaves out of us. Everyone wondered desperately about the other side.

"So," I said. "They got you next?"

Spyros nodded.

"Sure did."

Apparently, the disciples wedged a homemade explosive device into a crack in the building.

"Boom," Spyros said, opening his fingers. "Then came the bottles."

"Bottles?" I asked.

"Full of gasoline and fire."

"Oh," I said. Silence followed.

"Well," I said finally. "There's a dog out there for everyone."

"Yes sir," Spyros replied, not knowing what I meant.

He had a dog chasing him his whole life.

It caught him.

It was in the form of smoke inhalation.

28

Everyone was born with a dog on their heels.
Some people had faster dogs than others.
Spyros was thirty-seven when his dog caught up to him.
Bulgruf was sixty-five.
I was twenty-nine, in human years.

Habir's dog was not the cancer in his esophagus.
It was the barbed wire around his neck.

***

We were going to his apartment.
Habir told us there was a door leading to the roof, which was never locked. I thought it would be a good idea to go up there and scan the city. Seemed like the best way to find the arks. Bulgruf agreed with me. I have no idea what Flyes was thinking. Her pupils were different sizes. Her brain had deep bruises all over.

***

We splashed down the streets of San Francisco. They were flooded with rain and oil. Dead bodies floated, collecting against broken cars. Most cars were steaming, metal cages. The disciples did a good job flipping them over, setting them on fire.

Even the buildings were sinners, apparently.

Most of them were smoking piles of wood and brick. I was shocked at how much damage was done in five days.

And I remember the post office very clearly. Its windows were blown out, leaving squares of jagged glass. The front door was barred from the outside.

Inside there was fire, broken bottles, dead sinners.

Not to mention, plenty of late mail.

Another thing: the postmaster was outside. He had been shoved head-first into a trashcan.

I can see it now:

His legs dangled, swaying in the wind.

There were no pants or shoes. His feet were cut off.

His dog came in the form of water.

The trashcan was full of it.

***

Yes, it had been five days at that point. Five days since the beginning of my last adventure. I thought the afterlife would be an adventure. Instead, it's full of people who have no idea what to do, or where to go.

Might as well be Mother.

Time is different up here, though.

We have an awful lot of it to goof around with.

Back home, we had almost no time, and still goofed around.

The last time I saw a clock on Mother was at that post office. They had one out front. Its glass was broken, dripping with rain. The hands were stuck on four o' clock in the afternoon.

I wonder if the angels noticed that. They probably have no idea what time is, or why we used it.

I was looking at the clock when Habir said to me,
"They're burning people."
I looked over.
He was pointing across the street.
It was a sex toy shop.
They had an advertisement up. Everything was fifty percent off. That was a good deal.
A pair of human legs was dangling in front of that ad poster. The feet were shackled in furry handcuffs. The handcuffs were tied onto a long, sexy whip.
That whip was attached to the roof.

The other fifty percent of the person was hanging next to her own legs. A whip wrapped around her neck.
The person was charred black, steaming against the rain.

***

I still remember that. *"They're burning people."*
Habir had pretty good English for a towel head.
Somehow, his words followed me to Heaven.

Something else that followed me is Bulgruf's face when he saw the apartment building.
His mouth dropped open.
"You ok, big buy?" I asked.
"Sure," he said.

Now I realize something. The big man's heart was having trouble. He had seen this apartment before, about forty-one years prior.

It brought back bad memories.
And it was about to create a few more.

***

We waded through oil and water, across the intersection, to the front door.

I struggled with it, fighting the handle.

"Fuck," I said, "is it locked?"

"Yes," Habir said. "Locks when you close it."

I stepped back.

I was a fool.

Habir approached the door, patting his pockets for the key.

"Oh no," he said.

29

HABIR NEVER found them.

He was ashamed, I think. It is hard to remember much after that, but I can see him now. In the clouds before me, there is my terrorist friend, crying, apologizing with his whole body.

I see myself putting a hand on his shoulder.

I hear myself telling him it's ok.

Until that locked door, I had been high on THC or cloud paste or magic medicine.

Now, that was all gone. No more drugs.

Being sober for the apocalypse was a load of shit.

***

Here is a disclaimer: it has been two-thousand years since my death. My memory is broken into pieces, as they say. Those pieces are evaporating.

I might have already warned you about that, but I have no idea.

This is happening to a lot of souls.

Once, I saw a whole group lying down with their eyes closed. They were afraid of their histories. They were embarrassed. They were scared to lose the good times.

I sympathize.

Sometimes, I try to avoid the aether clouds too. I try not to think about anything at all. When I see my imagination, I feel fear, just like I did on Mother.
Even the good times are painted in distress.
I feel them leaving.

Two-thousand years is a long time for old memories.

Soon, you will need to question everything I say.
All of it may be false.

***

Sometimes, hindsight fights back.
It gets tired of being my slave.
Sometimes, it rolls around like a monster.

The clouds will be fuzzy and full of static. I'll see cracks, as if my memory is a broken screen. Something buzzes in there, buzzes and grinds all at once, like broken gears.
It's two machines making love, I think.

Sometimes the clouds show me everything at once.
I'll see Roselle tucking me in bed. There is a wall of water, three miles high. I step onto a train.

My mind tries to create memories because it knows I'm running out.
And it tries to fix the ones that are broken.
Sometimes, the clouds show me this:

I'll see two cities at once.
Both are San Francisco.
Both are outside the locked door of an apartment building. One is all concrete. The other has carpet.

Then, there are three visions at once.
I'll see the whole group, all four of us.

The first vision shows us running away from something.
We splash down the streets. I'm out of breath. Somehow, we
are inside a dumpster. Bulgruf passes out. Habir is missing.

The second vision is a bright light.
We are walking up a metal ramp, into a ship. There are
men in uniforms, keeping everyone in line. They are telling me
to stay calm. They look at my face, ask for my name. I tell
them. Somehow, I'm ok.
Habir isn't allowed onboard.

In the third vision, the disciples are surrounding us.
They were waiting around the corners. Our backs are against
the apartment door. Bottles burst into flames, we are pelted
with rocks. Habir is dragged away. I'm on fire, drenched in
burning gasoline.
I hear screaming.
Something about nine-one-one.

30

So, when my brain acts up, I just close my eyes.
Voila.
Instant privacy.
With closed eyes, I thank God for privacy.
I thank God for complete darkness.

And I wander with them closed.
I walk for miles.
I keep going because I don't get tired or thirsty.
I wonder who I am passing, who's memories are playing in the clouds around me.

Nero might be around, watching a city burn, just like I was.

Hitler might be around, watching the rain fall, just like I was.

***

I thought that if I walked forever, I would open my eyes and see that I accidentally strolled into Heaven. I would have missed the grand opening. That would be fine. I would still say hello to Nero and Hitler, and to Bulgruf and Flyes.
I would say hello to God.

I would walk outside again, just to tell Henry the Gates were open. Henry would smile, tell me to appreciate what I have. He would lie down forever.

***

Once, while I walked in complete darkness, I heard a song playing. It was in the distance, popping with static. Hindsight was telling me it came from a broken-down car.

Was that true? I have no idea. Though, I doubt there are many cars outside Heaven.

But what do I know.

Maybe it was a police siren. Might have been Flyes singing with her friends. Or, it was a turntable, grainy and full of charisma.

Then, it disappeared.
It was replaced by a human's voice:

"Howdy, partner," it said.

I opened my eyes.
It was Henry, lying on the clouds.
Somehow, I made it all the way back to him.

"Henry?" I asked.
"Yes?" He said.
"Where am I?"
"Not Heaven," he said. "That's what they tell me."
I rubbed my forehead.

"Troubled mind?" He asked.
I nodded, closing my eyes again.

The old farmer patted the clouds next to him. It was an invitation to sit and enjoy myself.

"Who's the troublemaker?" He asked.
"Me," I said. "I am the troublemaker."

He smiled. The clouds above him had changed since last time we saw each other. They had become a sunset. It looked real.

"Henry," I said, "what's happening to me?"

"Whatever you want," he said.

"I want to go to Heaven."

"Then go."

"Jesus, Henry," I said. "It's locked, remember? The Gates are locked."

We were silent for a while. I had been an asshole.

"Sorry," I said. "You're a nice guy, Henry."

He smiled, looking at me.

"Tell that to God," he said.

***

Henry told me that God had been walking around outside Heaven. Said a few others spotted Him, started to spread the word. But, whenever people ran to catch up, they landed back at the Gates.

"Everyone keeps going in circles," he said, twirling his finger. "They say no matter where you walk, you end up at God's front door. Folks don't know if they're crazy or not." Henry looked at me, said, "Good for them. Good for the crazy ones. Might keep them busy for a while, 'till the doors swing open."

I thought about that.

"They're not crazy," I said. "It just happened to me. I was walking as far as I could in the other direction." I pointed to the distance.

"Really?" Henry asked.

"Really," I said.

"And you landed back here?"

I sprinkled my fingers, showing that I was present.

"No shit," he said. "Well, *you* might be crazy."

About Henry: He actually was insane on Mother.

I know because he made me talk to his dead father.

On Henry's farm, two-thousand years ago, I introduced myself to an invisible man. I had to shake hands with him and say, *"Pleasure to meet you."*

It pleased Henry a lot. Apparently, it was his father's eighty-sixth birthday.

Back then, Henry said his old man wasn't the talkative type, and that I shouldn't expect a reply back. I told him not to worry about that, my expectations were very low.

It would not surprise me if some of that insanity had followed Henry to the afterlife.

***

I had no idea what to do next. In that moment, sitting next to a lonely, old man, I saw how long the afterlife was.

"Hopeman," Henry said, "why are you fighting?"

"Fighting what?"

"Yourself."

"I'm not."

He smiled, shaking his head. The sun was getting lower, painting his farm gold.

"Your mind is trying to have sympathy for you," Henry said. "Insanity is the best escape when there's no other way out."

"Sounds nice."

"It is nice," he said.

"Sounds like it," I said.

I closed my eyes again. No one spoke for a while.

"What's on your mind?" I asked.

He said, "Why don't you see for yourself?"

I told him my eyes were being private. I liked the darkness.

"Are you afraid?" He asked.
I told him I was not.
He said to be honest.

"Yes," I said.
"What scares you, so close to Heaven?"

It was a beautiful question.
The truth was that I almost cried, after that kind of question.
But I said, "The end of the world scares me."
"Still?" He asked.
I nodded.
"What does it look like?" Henry asked.
"Well, the closer I get to the end, the worse I feel. Sometimes I see everything at once. I can't tell which things were real, and which things never happened at all."

We were both lying under the sunset, resting on clouds.
"I'll watch, if you'd like," Henry said. "You aren't keeping those eyes closed forever."

He was right.
I couldn't ignore my problems for all eternity.
So, my hand found its way into his. That's what some men did on Earth, when they talked for a while.

Then, I opened my eyes.

31

THE CLOUDS flashed with color.

We were in a hundred cities, all at once.
All of them, San Francisco.

Henry told me to relax.
"You've been talking to a lot of people up here," he said. "Pretty sociable guy, if you ask an old farmer like me. I reckon you're clogged with everyone else's nightmares."
"So," he said, "relax. This is the fun part."
He was right, again.

I went deeper into my broken memories.
I focused on that concrete apartment, on my friends, on the city.
I was wet and cold. The sky twisted with blue and violet clouds, bleeding rain over the city. We saw a river flowing through my legs. Down the street, there was a naked body stuffed head-first into a trashcan. Rain drizzled down his bare legs.

I kept going. The aether crackled with sparks.

Habir couldn't find the keys.
Flyes was crying, one pupil bigger than the other.

Bulgruf was supporting himself, bent over, leaning on a fire hydrant. He was telling us that it was finally over. The world was over.

"The world, the world, the world, the world..."

Down the street there were people.
They were coming closer.
They had Molotov cocktails.

I took Flyes by the hand.
We splashed down the street, going anywhere. Bulgruf followed.
I glanced back.
There were people behind us.
We kept going, turned the corner.

Henry and I watched as I opened up a dumpster, hoisted Flyes over the edge.
She plopped in.

I looked at Bulgruf.
"No," he said.
We spent a few seconds arguing.
He shoved me against the dumpster, told me to get in.

I listened.
Bulgruf closed the lid over us.
Everything went black. Rain pelted the dumpster lid.
Sounded like butterflies, all with little drums.

***

Outside, there was chanting from dozens of voices.
Screaming, whistling, barking sounds.
That cocaine was good stuff.

Someone said, *"Thou shall not glut thyself, motherfucker."*

There was beating, splashing, and so on.
All of it, muffled by the sound of butterflies.

I pressed a finger against Flyes' lips.
It meant, *"Don't make a fucking sound."*
Blood drummed through my skull.
I closed my eyes, counting high as I could.
I counted the rain drops, as many as I could.
I might have been praying to God. I suddenly believed
in him again.

Then, the chanting died slowly.
It moved down the street, away from the dumpster.

Soon, it was gone.

There was only rain.

32

I HAVE NO IDEA how long we were in there.
It could have been an hour.
It could have been a year.

It was amazing what happened: Flyes and I passed out together. Yes, I was asleep in a dumpster with a dying angel.

Our brains had a lot of sympathy for us. They knocked us out with the sound of butterflies. Woke us up with the sound of butterflies. Everything in between was blank space. I had no idea what happened out there, what happened to Bulgruf. I had no idea what happened to Habir.

From inside, I cracked the lid open.
There was no one in the street.
Bulgruf was gone. The people were gone.
Habir was nowhere.

The aether showed me getting out of the dumpster.
Then I helped Flyes.
She stumbled, falling over nothing.
Her brain was shutting down.

We were standing in a river that used to be a backstreet of San Francisco.

A body floated by, face-down.

It had a pool cue in its ass.

***

Up in God's front yard, I looked away from the aether.
I told Henry I did not want to see the rest.
He smiled, patted me on the shoulder
That meant everything was ok.

So he thought of something beautiful instead.
It was a thunderstorm over the farm.
The sky was thick with deep, purple mist.
Lightning cracked through it.

I told Henry he was right. My mind was falling apart.
"Two-thousand years," Henry said. "Sure is a long time for memory to last."
I agreed.
He told me that other people had come by, other people he'd known from farmers' markets and the like. They sat down, spoke with him. Eventually, they got up, left.
"And I tell you," Henry said, "they're all crazy up there." He tapped his head. "All of them. Some worse than you."

Henry told me about a whole group of visitors.
It was other farmers he used to trade with.
Apparently, they were desperate. They wanted to know how Henry was staying so comfortable.
"They told me their imaginations were full of storms," he said, "full of screaming. One of them, every time he opened his eyes, he saw his wife getting crushed by a wall of water. Another one saw himself drowning over and over again."
"So," Henry continued, "I gave them my prescription."
I asked what that was.
He told me we were doing it right now.
"One dose of relaxation," Henry said, "it's got a half-life of forever."

It was true. I was comfortable.

We sat in the storm for a while, getting lost in the deep mist.

"And," he said, "I never saw those folks again."

33

THERE ARE THINGS I have left out from my past.
Things I have not told you.
Things I never will.

It's not my fault. My mind is the troublemaker.
I wish it would be reasonable.
I wish it would be honest.

But it's a part of my human soul.
And if I remember anything, it's that humans like me had a hard time being honest.

So, for the sake of honesty, I will say everything that comes to mind.
It might be garbage. As I said, I no longer have control over what my imagination decides to show me, true or false.

Up in the clouds, sitting next to an old farmer, my brain forced me into the memories of another man:

It was jamming the replay button on Bulgruf's history.

Yes, it showed me something I had forgotten about.
It was something Bulgruf told me a while ago, when we met by the Gates.
Henry and I watched as Bulgruf's dog caught up to him.

***

The man was on all fours.

He was face to face with the river. It flowed under him, carrying away blood that dripped from his face.

Bulgruf's left eye was black.

A red line trickled from his ear, down his cheek, dripping into the street.

Disciples surrounded him

They were holding knives and bricks. Someone had a baseball bat. It was wrapped in barbed wire. Another person had bare fists, covered in Bulgruf's blood.

They all had cocaine melting their brains.

And I saw how much they drooled.

It's true.

One woman stared at Bulgruf with wet, bared teeth and wide eyes.

Those eyes followed me into Heaven.

They were cracked-dry, bulging with red vessels.

She held a piece of glass so tight, her fingers were dripping red.

When Bulgruf told me all this, he said he was amazed by their clothes.

Everyone still had on their best Sunday outfits. I saw collared shirts, dresses. There were khakis. San Francisco was full of well-dressed believers.

They were soaked, covered in blood and dirt and rain.

Some people drooled over themselves, mouths stuck open, teeth exposed. Their pupils were twitching, stuck at different sizes.

I think that holy water did its job.

***

The disciples circled Bulgruf.

He was in the center, on all fours. A river flowed under him. There was a dumpster, somewhere to the side.

Then I saw another man.

He was holding a forty-five caliber revolver to Bulgruf's forehead.

The man was wearing a mask. It was a white hockey mask with a swastika scribbled in black marker. Next to that was the word *"Amen."*

Anyway, that mask certainly gave him authority.

The other disciples backed off, refrained from tearing Bulgruf in half.

The man in the mask said something.

He clicked the pistol's hammer.

34

Henry asked me what it sounded like.
I told him I couldn't remember, my brain passed out.
By the time I woke up, everyone had left.

"Big guy was gone?" Henry asked.
"Yep," I said.

The city looked empty. The apocalypse might have blown over while we were in that dumpster.
"And then you left?" Henry asked.
I told him we did. Told him how Flyes stumbled out, splashed face-first into the street.
"Poor girl," he said.
"She was going down anyway," I said, "brain was going down."
"Yep," he said. "We all were."

Henry asked where all those people went, where Bulgruf went.
I told him I had no idea. My memory was skipping that part. I guessed they had dragged him down the river, stuffed him inside something. The disciples loved stuffing bodies into things.

"Blank tape," I told him, tapping my head. "But, I know what he said before he died."

Apparently, the disciple asked Bulgruf for any last words.

Bulgruf said, "Fist me, doctor."

***

I asked Henry if he really met the High Priest, Arthur Sullenous.

"Sure did," he said. "Showed up on the farm, not long after you left."

Henry told me all about it.

Back then, he was on the front porch, ready to watch the end of time.

"Oceans falling from the sky," Henry said. "Beautiful, twisted clouds. Think they were dark blue, maybe purple. Mother never looked so good."

The farmer was wrapped in a blanket. He held a coffee mug close to his heart, felt the heat going through his shirt. There was an ashtray nearby. It was a graveyard of homemade cigarettes.

"Saw something down by the fence," Henry said. "Like a ghost. Pale as anything. Thought it was a skeleton coming for me."

Apparently, it was the most famous man in the world, the murderer and college dropout.

"Arthur A. Sullenous," Henry said. "Fell face-first into the mud."

That much is true.

Inside the priest's skull was a galaxy of liquor and cocaine.

"Said to myself, *'well, Henry, you can't just leave him there.'*"

So the farmer went down by the fence. There was a white, old man lying on the ground, covered in mud. He wore nothing but loose underwear and a massive erection.

Henry looked at me, separating his hands to demonstrate how long it was.
"Impressive," I said.
He nodded.

***

Then, they were in the farmhouse.
"I knew he was coming, figured he might be soaked. So I had a change of clothes ready for him in the bedroom. But the poor guy didn't even make it to the second floor."

Arthur threw up all over the stairs
He slipped, cracked his head on a step, tumbled down.

"Never thought I'd have a priest in my kitchen," Henry said. "At least not one who was naked and crying. Not in a pile of vomit, telling me how sorry he was."

Henry went on about why the priest was there in the first place. Said that before he was a holy man, Arthur was in a deadly car crash.
Henry told me that his parents died in that crash.
"So, Arthur came to apologize," he said, "must have found my name in a magazine, or something. Wrote to me. Told me he was coming for atonement. Said something about being unforgivable."
"When he showed up," Henry said, "the poor guy told me how sorry he was. Said something about not sleeping in forty years."
"What did you say?" I asked.

Back then, Henry looked at his invisible father and shrugged. He had no idea what the priest was talking about.

"Guess I had forgotten about the crash," Henry said. "I thought *he* was the crazy one. So I cleaned him up, wrapped him in something dry. We had soup, called it the last supper. I thought that was clever."

"And," Henry said, "those were the last vegetables I would ever take from the garden. Potatoes, corn, some other good stuff. Can't remember now. All with the special ingredient."

"Cloud paste?" I asked.

Henry nodded.

"And some home-rolled goodies," he said, touching an invisible joint to his lips. "I had him ready for the apocalypse. I had him ready for two."

Henry told me that darkness fell over his two-hundred acres. There wasn't a light for miles.

It was Mother.

"What then?" I asked.

"We went on the back porch. Talked for a while. Arthur said something about wishing he could do it over. He suddenly wanted to farm." Henry smiled. "I told him he could have mine."

They smoked for a while, listening to the rain. There was a soft rumbling in the distance.

"I still hear it. Still see the darkness," Henry said. "Everything was completely black. Couldn't see my own hands. But we thought to keep it that way. Never hung a lantern. Matter of fact, we didn't move for the rest of our lives."

I asked what came next.

Henry looked at me.

It meant that I already knew what came next.

35

WE WERE QUIET.
Henry had snow falling over his farm.
Mother was being gentle.

"What's the story this time?" I asked.
He told me there was no story.
He told me to imagine a cup of coffee in my cold hands.

I obeyed, feeling the warm ceramic.
Snow fell in blankets over the hills, the trees. I saw the truck, dressing up in white. Henry was wrapped in a wool blanket.

"Thank you," I said.
"For what?" He asked.
"For cooling my brain. You are made of cloud paste, Henry LaFelle."
He smiled, sipping his invisible coffee.

I told Henry that God should pay him a visit.
"He could use some cloud paste," I said.
"We all could," he replied.
I pressed my hands against the warm mug.
"God should apologize to us," I said. "We're the ones who had to be human."
Henry nodded, said I might be right.

"I had a good time," he said. "Can't blame anyone for that."

"I know. God bless you, Henry LaFelle."

***

The farmer asked me if I missed her.

"Miss who?" I replied.

"You know who," he said. "You were cute together. Couple of young birds."

"Oh," I said. "Yes, a little. I can see her anytime, though. It's hard to miss your friends when they live forever."

Henry agreed with me.

"Then tell me," he said, pointing to the snowfall, "what's all that about?"

It was Flyes.

The woman was standing outside the farmhouse, wrapped in a blanket.

She was holding a mug, just like me. I saw her walking slowly through Henry's imagination. Snowflakes melted on her face.

"No idea," I said.

"Well," Henry replied, "that's not *my* memory."

He was right.

It was mine.

My head was doing monkey business again, sparking and rattling without consent. It projected Flyes. I imagined her in Henry's daydream. I have never seen Flyes walk through the snow, but there she was.

Everything is monkey business.

Hindsight is a liar.

"Apologies," I said. "Can't help it."

Henry waved his hand. It meant there was no need to apologize any more.

"Tell that to God," I said.

***

Hindsight tells me everyone was the same, back home.

God made us all from the same stuff.

No one was really smarter than anyone else. At least, not when compared to God. And we all lived the same number of human years. At least, compared to God.

I know Henry LaFelle must have died peacefully in his home, two-thousand years ago. I bet a wave, three miles high, swallowed his farm. That's how almost everyone died. Some people were killed by the congregation in San Francisco, California. Others died naturally, or from cancer. Some people loaded nine-millimeter pistols and shot their families to death.

That reminds me of a family that walked by. There were four of them, all waving to us.

I thought it was nice.

They were walking together, stepping on patches of aether clouds.

They all had holes in their heads.

***

"I wonder if anyone made it," I said.

"Made it?" Henry asked.

"Yeah, onto the arks."

"Oh," Henry said. "I doubt it."

"Why's that?" I asked.

"Well," he said, "they didn't exist."

36

I WAS SILENT for a while.

"Well, Henry," I said, closing my eyes. "You fooled me."
"Yes sir," he said. "Figured you were better off with something to die for. When you three walked into my kitchen, I knew there was nothing left in the world. Nothing in the whole, goddamn world you wanted to fight for."

I realized I was still holding hands with him.

"But when you left," he said, "there was something like a fire."

"Thanks," I said.
He nodded.

The snow was still falling on Henry's farm.
At least, I think it was. My eyes were closed.
I was tired of watching Mother.

Henry asked if I wanted to hear a story.
"Sure," I said.

***

It was something Henry remembered from his teenage years. A book he read, or something.

Anyway, the story took place on a planet called Helven VI. It was in the Andromeda galaxy, two and a half million light years from Earth.

The citizens of this planet were called Helvians. They had very round chests, since they were born with large hearts. Their heads were big too.

Helven VI was in a crisis: its citizens were growing up to hate each other.

Helvians despised each other for being too rich or too poor, or being too dark-skinned, as some of them were. Helvians came in many colors. The common ones were purple, red, yellow, and dark blue.

The planet was billions of years old. Helvians had only lived there for a few hundred-thousand years. Since then, everything was powered by liquid water. Tanks, guns, bombs. Even televisions and vibrators. They were aqua-fueled. Helven VI was blessed with liquid water, but it did not have much. So, countries dredged deeper and deeper into the planet to find more.

They did eventually find more.

They even sucked up clouds and condensed them into vats of water. When they had to, they sucked up water from the roots of trees and plants.

Some Helvians were peaceful. They did not understand why everyone kept up the nonsense of war. They proposed that hate be swallowed, with a nice glass of water.

In one chapter, a whole family of innocent Helvians was cuddled around dinner. Their house was powered by water. In the scene, it was late afternoon, and everyone was home from school and work. The television was on, using up gallons of water. As the family sat down to eat, the screen turned into breaking news. It showed the severed heads of prisoners in some faraway place. The news anchor said,

"One hundred captives executed despite paid ransom."

The screen showed a pyramid of heads, all of them sawed at the neck. Blood spilled down the pyramid, making puddles. Obviously, the Helvians who did this had either no skill, or no regard, for design. The ordeal must have taken hours.

One of the heads died with its eyes open. It was looking at something far away, maybe at what the world had become. No one would ever know what he saw in those last moments. It could have been a bird. Helven VI had lots of birds. He could have been looking at the men who cut his head off. Maybe he was trying to forgive them.

He might have just been looking for his home.

The story continued.

Disaster grinned down upon people through their television sets. Children went to bed wondering what the next tragedy would be. Parents went to bed wondering how to keep their children safe.

Of course, the planet itself was fighting back.

After all, it had been abused. Every time a pile of bodies was burned, or a bullet fired, the atmosphere suffocated on smoke. It coughed on the offense of wasted water. Helvians were surgical in their disposal of waste: they sliced open parts of the planet and dumped remains inside. Bullet casings, smoldering cars, severed heads, some with their eyes still open —all of it shoveled underground. The world was infected. Trees sparsely grew, and when they did, their fruits were small and poisonous. Oceans began to drift away in slow, sticky tides.

But that is not what killed the Helvians.

The first thing to consume them was not war or planetary suicide.

It was no bullet, no polluted fruit, no storm.

Helven VI was dead with Fear.

It moaned in their beds every night. Helvians shared a pillow with it.

Fear waited for them, invisibly, at the kitchen table every morning. It was in their cars when they left for work. By the time they got home, it was resting with its legs on the ottoman. And, when dinner was served, Fear walked into the room and sat next to everyone at once.

***

The scientists of the world tried hard to reverse all that. They knew something had to give people courage, lest everyone kill themselves. So, scientists put all their brainpower together. They developed hundreds of serums, things to help the brain fight Fear. The scientists invented machines to rewire brains. They produced memory chips to delete trauma. Hundreds of subjects volunteered—all of them failures. Machines overloaded, melting their subjects. Memory chips malfunctioned, deleting everything. These unfortunate volunteers were never seen again.

Some solutions had no effect at all. The people walked out just as scared as when they entered. Desperation lingered in the laboratory like a deep fog. The scientists removed their glasses, their heads falling into cupped hands. No one spoke. They were berated enough by failure.

In that fog of shortcomings, the scientists tried one last thing.

With all remaining resources, they invented a pill.

The pill was free, of course, to everyone. One per person, one dose each. Its half-life alone was two-hundred years.

They called it *Indiferex.*

It decreased the sensation of emotions. The Helvians' response to fear would be so diluted that nothing could daunt them. There were no test subjects this time, no volunteers. No time to double check anything—the rate of suicide in the world was increasing every day.

So, one morning, an announcement was broadcasted over every radio and television station:

"This just in, Indiferex to hit the shelves in twenty-four hours. Cure the common fear with our miracle drug, free to all."

The next day, entire neighborhoods were deserted. No house would respond to the ring of a doorbell. There were also no cars—all of them had been driven to the grocery store, or the pharmacy, or wherever Indiferex was being given. Lines of Helvians stretched out of doors, all of them waiting for the same thing. When everyone got home, they sat down at their tables and opened the medicine, swallowed it.

Afterwards was quiet.

Everyone looked around at each other.

Nothing felt different.

That night, they went to bed thinking about their lives and their to-do lists. They thought of everything at once, the way Helvians did when they couldn't fall asleep. Some looked out their windows. There were an awful lot of stars in the Andromeda galaxy.

The Helvians tried counting them. They kept getting higher and higher until finally, the whole world was asleep.

***

The next morning, everything glowed in dim, yellow sunlight. All the cars and windows reflected golden fire. The homes, warm as always, powered by water, were silhouettes against the waking sun. A few birds had been singing.

Slowly, the world was awake.

Helvians ate breakfast, watched television, drove to work. They talked with their friends at lunch. They discussed the weather, and all joked about quitting their jobs. By sunset, everyone had driven back home. For once, life was normal. Normal was a relief.

They sat down for dinner and watched television.
The news was not very interesting.

When dinner was over, they went to bed.
The stars were out, as usual.
They were beautiful, as usual.

Nobody tried to count them.
Everyone just fell asleep.

The next morning, everyone got up. Breakfast, into the car, work. There was not much to say once they got there. They smiled a bit, nodded. Soon it was time to leave: back in the car, home. They smiled at their families. There was not much to say.
Dinner was served. Television was on.
Soon it was bedtime again. Stars again.
They were great. And the world fell asleep.

Soon, murders ended. No one wanted to kill any more.
Helvians still went to work for a long time. However, they really did run out of things to say. Jokes were hollow too. They were the last thing to get murdered.

Dinner was nice, and tasted the same every day. It was nice to trade chaos for consistency.
Also, traffic began to wane. Cars simply stayed home. People didn't feel like driving any more. Bosses came to their jobs, saw no one, and thought, *"What a shame."* They too, drove home for the last time.

Soon, people really did run out of things to say.

Families spoke to each other less and less, until without realizing it, they said their last words.

One day, the Helvians stopped getting out of bed.
Sunlight blared through windows, landing on unmoved laundry, unchanged calendars.

There was no hurry.

It was the last day that anything happened.

Every morning the sun began to shine a little less, because no one cared. So it died, its light going cold, by and by.
The birds flew away to other planets. On their way out of the atmosphere, there was no singing. Or perhaps, they sang as wildly as they could, one last time, but no one noticed.

In the last chapter, Helven VI floated away into space, no one caring about anything, feeling anything, doing anything at all. The scientists, too, never thought about anything else.

Indiferex was good stuff.
Finally, no one was afraid of anything.

37

I LOOKED at Henry.
We were still holding hands.

I told him the Helvians should have invented arks.
He agreed with me.

***

We said goodbye soon after that.
I stood up, brushed invisible dirt off my clothes. Henry told me not to spill my coffee. It was still hot, sitting in the invisible mug. I had set it down on the clouds.

"Great," I said, "God's going to be pissed I didn't use a coaster."
"Tell him it's my fault," Henry said.

I took his hand, said that I hope the Gates open soon, and that we meet again.
The farmer agreed, said he had a good feeling about that.

I smiled at him.
"God bless you, Henry LaFelle."

***

So I left.

Somehow, Henry was happy. He said I could find happiness too. I believed him.

Walking away, I imagined a rearview mirror. I thought I saw trees in it, and a farmhouse. There was a man, getting smaller and smaller.

He disappeared.

Yes, my imagination was rampant. Still is. Always will be. There will always be static and broken glass up there, floating around in my head.

Henry said so.

He was the one who taught me about insanity, showed me what it looked like. First on Earth, then in the clouds. He showed me that anywhere is Heaven, if that's what you want. Showed me that anywhere is Hell, if that's what you want.

Apparently, I wanted Hell most of the time.

On Mother, we were no good at telling the difference.

We loved Heaven most when it was already gone.

I thought about that on my way to the Gates.

That's where I was going, after all, to find Flyes. I wanted to see her, maybe we could find happiness together.

It wouldn't take long to get there. Apparently, everywhere lead back to the Gates.

That was ok.

At least I had friends.

She aged well, by the way. After two-thousand years, Flyes is as beautiful as the day we met. She is naked and bloody. Her pupils are still different sizes, and she has scars on her feet. I'm glad the ground up here is soft.

Like me, Flyes appreciates darkness. She shuts her eyes often. Apparently, her mind is a troublemaker. It tells her the clouds are made of broken glass.

Here is something I forgot to tell you:

Flyes has been naked and bloody for two-thousand
years.
So have I.

For a while, that was a big mystery to me.
I really forgot what happened.

Of course, the clouds lied to me.
Hindsight lied to me.

So I kept walking.

38

ANOTHER THING about God's front yard:
The Gates stretch up forever.

And, like I said, white mist floats out. Can't see over, or through. And, no matter where you go, it leads back to those Gates.

I don't think God wanted us to forget about the apology we owed him.
If we wandered too far, we might find Hell.
We would be so bored, we might knock on the door.

***

I saw that family of four again.

I said hello, tried not to look at their heads.
The dad asked me where I was going.

"To Hell," I said.

The others didn't have much to add. It was two children, and their mother. They were holding hands, looking at the clouds. Inside was an evergreen tree, decorated with lights. There might have been a fireplace.
The father told me about God.

Apparently, He'd been out here, wandering around, just like everyone else.

"Captain goes down with his ship," I said.
For a second, I heard butterflies.

"I guess so," the dad said. "I wish the Captain would take us to shore."

I smiled, wishing I had thought of that.

"You don't look so bad," he said to me, "not like the rest of them."
"The rest of them?" I asked.
"Well," he said, "we've seen folks with bones sticking out, feet missing. One poor guy had barbed wire around his neck."
I told him to peek inside my head. That might change his mind.
Of course, my brain would look like wet oatmeal.

"What a shame," he said.
His head also had a problem. There was a big hole in it. I could see all the way through. His family was on the other side, walking, holding hands. They were imagining an old photograph from the beach.
They all had holes in their foreheads.

***

It was true about my brain.
It was slush.

I thought Flyes might be able to tell me why. Maybe she still remembered how we died.
Or maybe not.
Her skull was full of slush too.

But I walked blindly, rolling through purgatory on two feet. I was grateful for them. Some people had theirs cut off. Some had theirs wrapped in leathery scars.

I thanked God for feet.

***

I found her, by the way.
Flyes' leathery feet were by the Pearly Gates.

"Hey," I said.
"Hey," she said back.
"Where are your friends?"
"On tour," she said, closing her eyes.
Apparently, they did not get enough attention back on Earth. They went off, singing for anyone that would listen, hoping to regain a following. They thought God would become a fan.

"Mind if I sit here?" I asked.
"No problem at all," she said back.

***

I told her about Henry LaFelle, how he had been sitting in the same place for two-thousand years.
"Sounds good to me," she said.
"He'd be happy to see you," I said back.
"I don't know," she said. "He was a lunatic."

The family of four walked by, waved to us. We waved back.
"We were all fucked up," I said. "But we didn't appreciate it the way Henry did. I guess I should have had more rapport with my dead dad."
She smiled, pretending to shake hands with an invisible man.

"Don't expect a response," I said, "he's not the talkative type."

"Don't worry about that," she said. "My expectations are very low."

***

I asked her about the last day on Earth.
She said she didn't like to think about that any more.

"Not provocative enough for you?" I asked.
"Something like that," she replied.
"Maybe we're all just in a dream," I said. "Or a coma."
We smiled at that, wishing it were true.

I apologized for there not being miles of trees up here.
She apologized for not being a beautiful wife.
"Sorry I didn't pick the strawberries," I said.
"Sorry I never made love to you," she said back.

I thanked God for my lack of penis.
I wonder if he heard how much we apologized.

***

I also wondered if I would get a penis in Heaven.
I wondered if I would have one when I got stuffed inside a new body. At the time, I was not in a position to ask God for favors. Still, I turned around, put my lips between the bars.

"Please, God," I asked, "don't let me be a woman next time."

Flyes smiled. She cupped her hands over her mouth, asking me in God's deep voice, what I would like to be instead.

"A cat," I said.

***

180

Flyes had been having flashbacks.

She told me her brain was full of broken glass, just like mine.

I thought about saying, *"At least you didn't step on it."*

But I was quiet. I listened to her as if we were a brand new couple. I listened to her the way Henry listened to me.

"My memory has no idea what it's doing," she said. "It's in pieces. It reflects off those pieces in a million different directions."

I told her that was ok.

Told her to let it all out.

***

Flyes' imagination crackled to life.

We saw a black wall crushing through San Francisco, California. There was a young woman in the streets, giving someone a blow job. The woman had a tattoo on her collarbone.

Then there was a dumpster. It got hit by a train. When she opened the lid and crawled out, Flyes found herself in a kitchen. There was breakfast ready. Everyone was eating bowls of broken glass, washing it down with rum and vodka.

When she sat down to eat, she was looking out the windshield of a truck. It was raining. The windshield was a force field of running water. The water had cocaine in it.

She was lying on her mother's shoulder, in the front seat of a pick-up truck. Her mother was telling her the story about how she found a tapestry. There was a hobo involved, and a bag of fake dollar bills.

The hobo was in a coma.

He was dreaming about being stuck in Heaven forever, with nowhere to go. He tried to jump off the clouds, fall into space, and die.

But someone talked him off the edge.

Then, that hobo became a priest, and killed all the other hobos who were sinning.

But Flyes was the hobo the whole time.

She crawled back into the dumpster.

"Then I close my eyes," she said.

"And what do you see?" I asked.

"Nothing," she told me. "Sometimes, I thank God for nothing."

39

IT WAS MY TURN.
I opened my eyes.

There were gunshots.
I was in my bedroom in Oakland, California.
Downstairs, an old terrorist had been shot in the chest five
times. Everyone hated him because he was too dark-skinned.
He was from a planet where everything was powered by water.
Soon, that water swallowed everything.
Then there was a pool cue in my anus.
I couldn't get it out.
I gave up. I lied down in the streets of San Francisco,
and let the water carry me away.
I passed by a man getting shot in the face.
He was dragged into the back of a semi-truck.
Next, I floated by three men who were holding each
other's penises.
They were on fire, and drinking coffee.
A handsome man was serving them coffee. He had
smoke blowing from his mouth and ashes on his face.
Then I stopped floating. I got caught against a
dumpster. A beautiful woman crawled out of it, falling face-
first into mud. She had a galaxy of liquor and cocaine in her
skull.
She was helped up by an old man.
He took her into his home, cleaned her up.

Then, they sat on the porch all night, watching a snowstorm.

There was lightning.

I saw someone getting dragged through the snow. He was a college student, with no facial hair. He was plopped into a car.

I was in the car when it drove away.

I saw the porch in the rearview mirror.

The drunken woman was there, with her savior.

They were sitting on the porch.

They were upside down.

Their chairs were upside down.

They were both bleeding from the nose.

40

We sat for a while without talking or thinking.
That was fine.
Sometimes it was comfortable to be braindead.

That's what happened, after all, when you pushed through the broken glass of your memories. Everything got heavier, and deeper. Felt like walking through a river. Then that river turned to mud. Then it turned to stone.

"And then," I said to Flyes, looking at her, "then you're dead up there."

She smiled, put her fingers into the shape of a pistol. She put the pistol against her head. She pulled its invisible trigger. Her invisible brains popped out. It looked like wet oatmeal.

We talked with useless, lazy sentences.
It was nice to just hear each other.
It was nice to say anything without judgment.

I was convinced the only person left who wanted to judge us was God himself. And I was convinced He was not around. He certainly wasn't listening. He was probably just as bored as we were.

So the two of us spoke carelessly.

Her mouth wrote long, cursive sentences about the end of Heaven. She told me a story about a wall of clouds that would swallow everything up here. It would be three miles high.

"Where next?" I asked.

"Next?" She said.

"Yeah," I said, "where would we go next?"

"Earth," she said, thinking about it. "The angels would have to clean this place up. But Mother wouldn't want us again, so she'd send another big wave. And then God would have to send his angels back there again to clean up. And no matter where we went, someone would be angry at us."

"I'm sorry, Mother," I said.

"I'm sorry, God," Flyes said.

No one ever apologized to the angels.

They had to clean up everyone's mess.

***

I remember asking Flyes to walk with me.

"Why?" She asked.

"Why not?" I replied. Said I had been walking for two-thousand years. There was no chance of getting lost.

"No chance," I said. "And so what if we do?"

She told me there was nothing to do out there.

I told her it was better than being a groupie.

So we walked for a while.

We even held hands.

When I put my hand over hers, she asked why.

I told her that's what people did sometimes.

"We never did that," Flyes said.

"Sure we did," I told her.

She said to prove it.

"Look at the clouds with me," I said. "And I'll prove it."

So we walked for miles, watching Mother through a broken screen. San Francisco was in pieces. It was fuzzy with static.

But somehow, when I walked next to her, the pieces fit back together.

And when she took my hand, the static was gone.

41

THERE WAS A DUMPSTER in San Francisco, California.
I helped Flyes crawl out.

She splashed face-first into the street.
"Jesus," I said, trying to help her. "You ok?"
Her knees wobbled.
She looked at me with two wild pupils.
"Flyes," I said, shaking her. "Do you hear me?"
The woman nodded. She was limp in my hands.

And she was limp, wobbling towards her fate.
The clouds showed us sloshing through the city, walking
down empty streets.
We couldn't run.
We tried.
Flyes stumbled over nothing, falling over and over.
I was running out of breath.

So we were steady.
We moved when we could, hid when there was a noise.
I remember crawling face-down under a pick-up truck.
Its bed was loaded down with furniture and a television. There
was a refrigerator too. It made the truck too heavy to flip.
The driver was dead in the front seat.
His upper torso was sitting there, hands on the steering
wheel.

His legs were in the passenger seat next to him, resting comfortably. The windows were splattered with blood.

It was all very creative.

We were under that creativity when disciples sloshed by.

I saw their feet splashing, kicking up water. They stood still for a moment. The river flowed over their Sunday shoes, rushing through their legs.

I closed my eyes, put a finger against Flyes' lips.

Rain pelted the metal truck.

It was every butterfly, falling from Heaven.

Hindsight tells me I really believed that.

Every sinner who died that day came back, just for a few moments.

They got to fly around as butterflies.

The disciples must have decided the area was purified.

They took their Sunday shoes down the street, around the corner, gone.

***

We kept going, moving onto the next street. I was looking for any signs of life. Flyes stumbled along.

Then, we stood still. We were on the sidewalk, in front of a library that would not burn down. It was marble, through and through. It looked unharmed. Rain washed down its smooth, white walls. They went up an awful long way into the sky. It seemed like a waste of stone.

But I was thankful.

I told Flyes we ought to see if we could get up there, to the very top. If the arks were around, they'd see us waving.

The marble steps leading to the front door were covered in bodies. We stepped over them, trying not to slip.

One of them had a pair of scissors stuck in its eye socket. That person died with their mouth open. Water pooled inside, bouncing with rain drops.

Another body was headless. It was wearing an unzipped backpack. Inside was the person's very own head.

At the top of the stairs, there was a marble archway crowning the main doors. The arch made a little foyer, and was etched with Latin words.

I remember what they meant in English:

Knowledge, free to all.

That's what Roselle told me, twenty years prior. We went there together a few times.

Now, that marble engraving was covered by a white sheet. The sheet was covered in black marker. The black marker said, in English:

Welcome to Paradise.

I tugged on the front door's handles.

The doors were massive, iron slabs, inlaid with polished wood. The wood was studded with more iron.

They didn't budge.

"Fuck," I said, bending over, hands on my knees.

It looked like the disciples had tried to get in.

There were hammers left by the door. There were dents in the wood, scars on the handles.

Then there was a voice.

It was a woman. She spoke from the other side of the doors.

"Business or pleasure?" she asked.

I looked at Flyes, who was looking at me.

We both had no idea what to say.

"Neither," I said, my face close to the polished wood.

There was silence.
A waterfall of rain was behind us, flowing off the archway, down the stairs. We were shivering in the cold wind.

Then it happened.
There were gears moving inside. Sounded like twisting metal, moving bolts.
It unlocked.

The door creaked open.
I saw dim lights inside.

Then a shotgun was pointed at my face.

42

A MIDDLE-AGED woman held it, finger on the trigger.

She was wearing a rabbit mask.

It had plastic ears sticking up, and a plastic smile. There were plastic eyes with little holes in them. Behind those holes, human eyes aimed down the barrel of a twelve-gauge shotgun. That barrel was two feet from my head.

"Welcome to Paradise," the bunny said. "How may I help you?"

I put my hands in the air slowly. It meant I was harmless.

"Nothing," I said. "We were just leaving."

"Nonsense," the bunny said, laughing. Her weapon swerved towards Flyes. "Come inside."

***

Aether says the inside of the library was dark, glowing with dim, red light. There were crimson lanterns hanging by chains and ropes. There were candles on tables and floors. A fireplace was lit, burning with old books.

Somewhere to the side, I heard a piano. A man was sitting at the bench, tapping his fingers over the keys. He had on a plastic goat mask.

Behind us, the doors locked again.

I turned around.

"Welcome, welcome, welcome," the bunny said, lowering her weapon. "You must be in the business of pleasure, coming to a place like this." She was dressed in a bathrobe. Hindsight tells me it was made of red silk.

I looked around.

There were people lounging over leather furniture, everyone with an animal mask and a bathrobe. Some people wore suits. There was a topless woman who wore a bearskin rug over her breasts and shoulders. She had a wolf mask. Her hair dangled in long, dark locks. One man was completely naked, sitting wide-legged on a furry couch by the fire. He had on a horse mask, and was fully erect.

The floors were marble too. In the center of the room was a huge fountain. It was surrounded by cauldrons of smoking incense.

"Please," the bunny said, "have a seat." She curled up on the bench next to her goat friend. He was still playing the piano.

Flyes and I were silent.

We sat down on a leather couch.

That couch was in the middle of the foyer, right by the piano. Hindsight tells me that every window in that place was boarded with old, wooden planks. They were high up, unable to be reached by anyone outside. No light came through. I heard thunder in the distance.

The ceiling was awfully high.

A chain hung from up there, dangling a chandelier.

It reflected the candles, scattering dots of yellow fire throughout the room.

"So," the bunny said, lifting a glass of champagne off the piano. It left a ring of moisture, glowing in the red light. "You don't look like everyone else."

I stared into her bunny mask.

I had no idea what stared back at me. She sipped the champagne, liquid spilling down her mask, over her bare chest.

"Right," I said. "I suppose you are right."

To my side, I saw a monkey and a cow playing chess. The pieces were missing. They were moving invisible soldiers.

"So, so, so different," the bunny said. Her shotgun was leaning on the piano. "Little girl," the bunny said, "what does your spirit tell you?"

I looked at Flyes.

She looked at me.

There was silence.

"Something," the bunny said, twirling her glass. "Something unbound."

The robed woman stood up, grabbing her weapon. She walked to a coat hanger by the front doors. It was hanging with various plastic faces.

"Something free," she said, lifting a dark mask. "Something born in the night."

The bunny stepped over to us, holding a raven mask. It had a long, dark beak. She slid the mask over Flyes' face. The bunny placed her plastic lips against the raven's beak, giving it a plastic kiss.

"And you, lovely," the woman said, walking back to the coat hanger. "What does your spirit tell you?"

I was silent.

I shook my head, meaning that I had no idea.

"I'm waiting, lovely," she said.

"Well," I replied. "I have no idea."

She pumped the shotgun, turned around.

It was pointed at my face.

"What do you see?" She asked.

Blood drummed though my skull.

"What," she asked, stepping closer to me, barrel locked between my eyes. "What animal do you see?"

I stared down into the gun.

I closed my eyes.

"A butterfly," I said.

43

THERE REALLY WAS a butterfly mask.
I couldn't believe it.
Apparently, there could have been any mask I wanted.
The bunny made mine from an old book.

So I was a butterfly.
The bunny stepped closer, crawled on top of me, slipped the mask over my face.
She pecked my cheek with a plastic, bunny kiss.

"Welcome," she said, returning to the piano bench. The goat was tapping another song. It was beautiful.
"Thank you," I said. "What is this place?"

She looked at me, tipping the last of the champagne down her mask. It dripped off the end, landing on her breasts.
"Paradise," she said, tilting her head to the side. She opened her arms, spreading them out, so as to reveal a masterpiece.
I looked around some more.

There was the naked man, smoking a pipe through his horse mask.
The monkey and cow were still playing invisible chess.
The wolf woman was twirling in slow, dramatic circles, moving with the sound of the piano.

I looked at the raven next to me.
She looked at a butterfly.

"We all live here," the bunny said. "It's a warm place for warm creatures."
She had bare feet.
They dangled off the bench, almost touching the marble floor. A line of champagne trickled down her leg, dripping off her big toe.
I looked at the shotgun, then back at the bunny.
"Thank you for having us," I said.
"Thank you for joining," she replied, staring at Flyes.
The bunny told us that there were a million worlds to explore, all of them in the books.
"Books are everything," she said. "We used to live as robots, working for the library. We were trapped in human bodies. But the apocalypse has delivered us. We have been reborn."
I watched her closely.
I knew about this library from when I was a boy. It was owned by the city of San Francisco. It employed disabled and handicapped people, young and old, to find opportunity in life. I did not know it hired animals.

"Reborn?" I asked
The bunny was silent. She nodded to Flyes.
"Raven doesn't talk much," the bunny said. "Does our raven not like her nest?"

"No, no," I said, patting Flyes on the shoulder. "Our raven is fine. She has had a hard day, that's all. We both have."
The bunny was silent.
She picked up the shotgun.

"Follow me," she said.
The bunny stood up, moved toward the center of the room. Her bare feet stepped over rose petals, pages from old

books. There were puddles of champagne and broken ashtrays. A giant candle was leaking hot wax all over the floor.

I followed her.

Flyes was right behind me.

The place smelled like the inside of a roasting joint.

Looked like it too.

Smoke floated in gray blankets, swimming through us like ghosts.

It was not normal smoke.

We stepped over the bodies of sleeping animals. They were dressed in wild, fabulous costumes. I saw a bee wearing a shower curtain. There was an enormous kitten. She had pink hair, tattoos, and was plastered with pages from old books.

"Mother of God," I said to myself.

***

The bunny stopped in front of the huge fountain.

It was in the center of the first floor. The first floor was now a mountain range of books. They had been stripped from their shelves, tossed in piles. Some piles had candles on top, illuminating the room with soft, yellow light.

The fountain used to be so beautiful in my childhood. It was warm copper, carved with intricate designs.

Now, it was dead.

The building no longer had electricity to sustain the poor fountain. There was not even water left in its green, decaying bowls.

The bunny turned around, looked at us.

She snapped her fingers.

From somewhere, a man in an elephant mask walked over to the bunny. He lowered himself onto one knee, presenting a silver tray. He lifted a silver dome from the tray, revealing an old perfume bottle. It was filled with dark syrup. That bottle had a rubber tube, which ended in a nozzle.

"Come," the bunny said, curling her index finger.
I obeyed.
I did not feel like myself. I was dizzy.

My brain had always been a traitor. I knew that. All my life, it told me everything was dangerous, and that the world hated everyone. But in that dark room, one day from the apocalypse, it told me the truth: the smoke in that room was not normal.
And that's what hindsight says too.
It tells me the smoke in the air was not from joints or cigarettes or incense.
I have no idea what it was, or what it did to me.
All I know is this: I did not feel like myself.

I wobbled over to the bunny.
She cupped a handful of invisible water from the fountain, doused it over my head, baptizing me.

She whispered, through plastic lips,
"Breathe deep."

The nozzle was slipped under my mask, between my lips.

The bunny squeezed a rubber bulb.
I inhaled.

44

My brain flashed with electricity.
It sizzled and popped like a pan of hot grease.
I saw something.
The room vibrated in soft ripples, as if gravity were letting go of me.

"What the fuck," I said, holding my face. It was numb.
Flyes did not feel like herself either.
She stepped up to the nozzle.
It went under her mask, into her lips.

***

My brain tripped over double vision.

The bunny pushed me.
I landed on a giant bean bag chair.
Flyes was next to me. Her head leaned back, mouth open.
She was breathing fast.

"You are reborn," the bunny said. She was climbing the fountain. "The apocalypse can take nothing from you now. You and your spirit have found each other."

I looked away from her.

I saw the mountains of books, and the candles on top.
Hindsight tells me I lost control.

"Someone's up there," I said, looking at the mountains. They were covered in snow. There was a light coming from them. "Someone's sending a signal."

"We see lots of things," the bunny said from atop the fountain. "See lots of things when we are reborn."

She was right.

I saw the first floor of the library become the Andes Mountains. The candles became flare guns. They were glowing in the distance. There was smoke.

"Bulgruf," I said, feeling my heart.
Hindsight tells me I floated off the chair, into space.

Then I was in the mountains, watching two people dangle from a cliff.

I thought someone was falling.
I thought someone else was letting go.

"Bulgruf, don't let go," I said, whispering to myself.
I looked over at Flyes. She was smiling, mouth open.
She looked like she was masturbating.
Hindsight tells me she really was.

"Jesus," I said, grabbing my face. I slapped Flyes' arm, trying to get her attention. She didn't care, she kept going.

"Flyes," I said, "stop it. We need to help him."
She didn't hear me.

I was in the Andes, screaming from the mountains.
I was a helicopter.
And I floated so close to Bulgruf.

He was wearing a bunny mask, standing on the highest peak, in the middle of the room.

Then, Bulgruf slipped the nozzle through his mask, took a deep breath.

He let go.

***

The bunny let go.
She fell from the fountain, cracked her face against the marble floor.

"Jesus," I said, sliding off the bean bag chair.
The world was upside down, then upright again.
Flyes was blasted from chemicals, masturbating herself to death.
My legs were made of water. They collapsed under me. I fell into the white, marble floor.
There were rose petals by my nose.

"Bulgruf," I said, drooling. I crawled closer to the bunny. She was lying still.

Her head was in a puddle of dark blood.
I inched closer, running out of breath.
A blizzard was searing my face, coating the mountains with thick snow.

I pulled myself next to her.
She was holding a broken perfume bottle.
It had shattered into a puddle of syrup and glass.
Her mask was smashed too, blood leaking out.

"Hopeman," she said, putting a finger against my cheek.
I slipped off her plastic bunny face.

It was Roselle.

45

Outside Heaven, we were still sifting through miles of soft clouds.

Flyes asked if that vision was true, if the bunny was Roselle.

"Doubt it," I said. "I don't trust anything I saw back then."

In the aether, we saw Roselle on the floor, blood leaking from her nose and ears. I tried to shake her to life, but there was none left.

No one cared.

None of the animals ever noticed.

"Circle of life," Flyes said to me as we watched the clouds.

"Circle of life," I replied.

She was right.

There was a white banner in that room, hanging over the fountain. It was scribbled with black marker:

Be reborn into the Circle of Life.

It was true that Roselle climbed to the very top, inhaled syrup, and dropped head-first into marble.

And it was true that I saw myself as a helicopter coming to her rescue.

But can I be trusted?

Well, I thought I was a helicopter.
I thought Bulgruf shot a flare gun in the library.
And I thought Bulgruf was Roselle.

***

Back to the library.

My brain was sizzling on cool acid.
I felt it bubble up my throat, out my mouth.
I splashed vomit all over those white, marble floors.

The aether was dizzy, just like me.
I looked back at the beanbag chair. Flyes was limp. There were two of her. They were both passed out, drooling.
I was surrounded by beautiful, dying woman.
Everything moved as slow as possible. I thought the world might have been stopping in time.
It might have been dead.

Above my dead nanny,
    next to a lake of drugs and blood and vomit,
    in the middle of the apocalypse,
everything went quiet.

My heart drummed.
It was going slow, then fast.
It jumped around and danced.

But it never gave up on me.
It would pump fifty-eight thousand more times.
Flyes' heart would pump that much too.

The goat playing the piano had a human's heart.
It would beat seventy more times.

A wall of marble would collapse onto him in one minute.

The piano would be dead.

So would the man who stuck a pipe bomb to the outside of the library.

He wouldn't run fast enough.

The pipe bomb would live for five seconds after it was stuck. The wall would live for five seconds.

Afterwards, a truck that drove through the broken wall would live for thirty seconds. It would plow through rubble, crash into a marble column.

The marble column would die on impact.
The wolf in bear skin would be in front of
that column.

The driver would die on impact.
His airbag would die too.

The column would collapse.

The second floor would fall to its death, just like the bunny.
The monkey and the cow would be crushed.
The horse and the bee and the kitten would be crushed.

The elephant's brain was slop. He sniffed too much vapor.

The bunny was already dead.
Her brain was on the floor.

The fountain was dry and dead.
All the water had evaporated.

The lights were dead.
All the electricity had been used up.

Soon, the ocean would crash through the poor library.

The waves were full of trash.
They had been dead for years.

The Milky Way was dead.
God never made anyone else to live there.

God might have been dead.
He might have died peacefully in His home.

I don't think He heard my prayer before I blacked out.
It was the last Sunday on planet Earth.

46

WHEN I LIVED IN OAKLAND, California, I heard a story I never forgot.

It followed me to the afterlife.

During the last world war, survivors discovered piles of old shoes. There were tens of millions of them. They were gross. They were full of dirt and worms. I'm sure some of them still had feet inside.

Hindsight tells me the story over again:
There was a flower who captured millions of people.
He hated the people because they were too rich, or too dark-skinned.

And the flower had access to the best technology in the world. It was all powered by water.

And he kidnapped the people, forced them out of their shoes, glasses, and clothes. They were forced out of their own hair, too. It was set on fire. The people were then forced out of their own dignity.
The flower forced them to sleep on cold, hard ground.
It might have been white, marble floors.

Well, the people were eventually strapped onto conveyor belts and rolled into furnaces.

At least it wasn't cold any more.

And the shoes were left in piles for time to deal with.

Time was supposed to deal with everything.

***

I woke up naked in the street.

Next to my face was a pair of shoes. They were beautiful, Sunday loafers. They were filled with living, human feet. Those feet were connected to a disciple who hated me. He hated everyone. The drugs in his brain made him want to murder human beings. Hindsight tells me water flowed over his beautiful shoes.

In the aether clouds, I was limp.

I was naked, face-up on the Golden Gate Bridge.

Worst of all, I had a four and a half inch penis.

And everyone knew it.

Flyes was next to me.

She knew it.

She was also naked. She must have seen my penis.

There was duct tape around her wrists. I looked down her naked body and saw a rope around her ankles.

It was connected to the back of a pick-up truck.

And I saw another rope.

It went from the truck to my own ankles.

My wrists were also wrapped in duct tape.

Then the truck drove forward.

It pulled me across wet concrete.

Shoes were walking next to me, sifting through the water.

The truck's taillights stared at me through the rain.
They were bright yellow.
The vapor in my head told me they were our guardian angels.
It told me they were pulling us away from danger.
Apparently, they pulled us slowly, letting our naked bodies grind over the street.

In the aether, I see Flyes crying.
She was face-down, sliding over rocks and broken car windows.

***

In the aether clouds, I saw the ocean.
The horizon was a line of black clouds
Except, it was not clouds.
It would be getting closer and closer.
That was Mother, out there, loading her gun.

Another thing about my naked body:
It was going two-million miles an hour.

It sure didn't look like it. The truck was slow, splashing through fallen rain. Above me, water poured over my raw face.
I looked up.
The sky was dark clouds, going two-million miles an hour. They were getting faster, twisting in dark shapes.
They had nothing to say to me.
I had nothing to say back.

***

The truck stopped. We were on the other side of the bridge.
I looked at Flyes.
Her face was peeling off.
It had been mauled by two miles of asphalt.

We both left a trail of skin and tissue down the most beautiful bridge on Earth.

The sky dumped water over our red, exposed muscles.

And we felt nothing.

That vapor was good stuff.

The truck's exhaust pipe belched fumes into the rain. I wondered if I would be expected to smoke that too. I would wrap my lips around the pipe, and suffocate.

Maybe Flyes would wrap her lips around it.

She would be good at that.

***

The driver got out, slammed the truck door.

He walked over to my limp body.

He looked down, said something about how lucky I was, said a chunk of concrete missed my head by a few inches. And my *"Whore friend"* was even luckier.

That was true.

The library collapsed over us.

Somehow we lived.

I didn't care. I didn't feel anything.

But it was true that Flyes was luckier.

A chunk of marble broke off, crashed between us.

It ripped a hole in her cheek.

Now we were naked, bleeding, hanging with dead skin.

I looked at my whore friend.

She was crying, tears and rain spilling down her bloody face.

I tried to look at her as long as I could.

It was supposed to mean, *"Everything is ok."*

***

We were surrounded by disciples.

They watched as the driver pulled two road signs from the back of his truck.

I was face-up in the streets of San Francisco, California.

I was powerless.

The rain told me how powerless I was. It washed over my raw skin. It might have been Mother whispering to me.

She might have been saying, "*Everything is ok.*"

***

Then I saw myself walking.

I was naked, my four and a half inch penis dangling in the wind. The disciples chained the metal road sign to my ankle. I was dragging it down some street in some city.

Was it a road sign? I think so. It was heavy. The chain tugged against my skin.

Was it San Francisco? I think so. I looked back, saw a crowd of disciples. They were towered by buildings.

The buildings were on fire.

But I have no idea about anything any more.

My imagination wants to believe certain things.

It tells me our chauffeurs were armed with bricks and pool cues. They had knives, I think. Someone had a fistful of broken glass.

One of them had a fireplace stoker. It was right behind my back, to make sure I never stopped walking.

So I didn't.

I stepped through Hell on two bare feet.

My shoes were gone.

They were in a pile somewhere.

At the end of the street was a high-rise apartment. It was tall and dark, made of black marble. It loomed over the rest of the city. It looked as though it had been carved perfectly from a volcano, then polished.

I remembered it from my childhood. That was where my father stayed when he was too busy to come home. He had the penthouse, all the way at the top.

One time he took me to work with him. We were in his office for five minutes, so he could answer voicemails. Then, we traveled the city. We ate hot dogs, saw a movie. The movie was about someone who saved the world. I was seven years old. I wondered if my dad could save the world.

We drove over the Golden Gate Bridge. A song came from the radio, telling us what a beautiful world it was.

I wish I remembered the words.

But I only remember the sky.

It was purple and orange.

The sun was falling from outer space. It lit the Pacific Ocean on fire. It covered the bridge in gold light. Somehow, there was no traffic. I begged my father to turn around and go back again.

So we did.

He even took me to another movie.

And that night I fell asleep in his high-rise apartment.

The next morning, he took me home.

It was the most time I ever spent with my father.

I was twenty-nine in human years the next time I saw those apartments.

I would be naked, chained to a metal pole. The pole would have a black and white sign that said, *"One Way."*

There would be vapor in my brain.

The vapor would tell me my father was up there, standing on his balcony. It would tell me he was looking down at the city, waiting for me.

Now, hindsight shows me the name of that building.

"Obsidian Tower."

The name was carved in stone, somewhere on the outside. But hindsight also tells me those letters were covered up by a big, white bed sheet. It flapped in the wind, like my penis.

The sheet was spray-painted with letters of its own. It had crude swastikas and peace signs. The letters said this:

"Golgotha."

***

We continued down the street, closer to that building.

I looked over at Flyes.

She was naked, on her hands and knees. A road sign was chained to her foot. A disciple was behind her with a sharpened pool cue.

We passed the old theater. It still had the same marquee from so many years ago. Its lights were broken and dead. The letters were arranged to tell us which film was playing that night.

I suddenly tasted hot dogs.

"Hey," I said, pointing to the theater. "Who wants to see a movie?"

A fist cracked my jaw.

I fell, splashing to my knees.

"You like that, bitch?" Someone said, fashioning his knuckles in my face. He was showing me where that solid punch came from, and that another one was loaded.

Blood trickled down my lips. I tasted warm, metallic salt.

I looked at the man, and said,

"Yes, I like it."

He punched through my front teeth.

Blood popped out, spilling down my chin.

"Anything else, fucker?" He said.

The aether clouds spiraled. It was my brain rolling over itself. It was covered in static, like a broken radio.

I looked at the man. His fist was ready.

I looked at him, my eyes tripping on double vision, going in circles.

I said, through broken teeth,

"Fist me."

47

Here is something I forgot to mention:

The Golgotha had a garden on its roof.

It was full of grass and palm trees. There was a wooden bench that looked over the ocean.

That marble tower was built in the human year of nineteen seventy-five. During construction of the top floor, a shipment of drywall and marble had gone off the Golden Gate Bridge. The driver was drunk at nine o' clock in the morning and drove through the railing, into the ocean.

But the developers made a blessing out of all that.

They planted grass and trees and flowers up there instead. It was all real. It was a garden floating above the coast.

No kidding.

The Obsidian Tower was right on the beach. You could sit up there and watch the ocean crash against American sand.

That's something I would do before I died.
Flyes would be there with me.

We would be hanging upside down, bleeding from our noses.

***

Flyes is a part of my hindsight.

Up here, walking on the sky, she tells me that I blacked out in the street.

"Really?" I asked.

She threw a fist into her palm, showing how hard I had been hit.

I dodged an invisible punch, threw a jab. It showed how tough I was.

Flyes told me they wrapped us in tarp, carried us all the way to the apartment.

Apparently, the truck was out of gas.

"That was nice of them," I said. "Did you like it?"

"Like what?" She asked.

"The tower," I said.

"Oh," Flyes said, "you mean Golgotha? Yeah, it was nice."

***

The aether showed us the front lobby. It was beautiful. The floor was dark marble, inlaid with exotic stones.

It was covered in bodies.

They were naked, just like me.

Some of them were alive, just like me.

But the building was dead.

Its power was out. It had no water.

Somehow, the disciples had pried the elevator doors open. The hatch went two floors down, into a subbasement.

Flyes' memory was cracking. It was fuzzy.

But I saw a man with a pistol.

The pistol was pointed at a janitor. It said, *"Pick up the shovel."*

The janitor was crying.

He picked up a shovel.

"Now," the pistol said, *"clean this place up."*
I saw the janitor shake his head. He was crying.

The disciple clicked the pistol's hammer.
That meant, *"Do it."*

Flyes and I watched as the janitor shoveled bodies down the elevator hatch.
Some of the bodies were screaming.
Some of them never stopped, even after they hit the bottom.

The lobby was clean.
The janitor was good at his job.

I saw a disciple dump a case of gasoline down the hatch. He lit a match, gave it to the janitor.

The pistol said, *"Drop it."*
The janitor refused. Tears spilled down his face. He shook his head.
The pistol pressed against the man's head.
It meant, *"Now."*

The janitor took the match.

***

"They carried us all the way up," Flyes said, holding my hand. "After the fifth floor, the screaming finally stopped. The smoke didn't."
She said the elevator shaft was a chimney.
"Oh," I said.
We were silent for a moment.
I imagined smoke belching from the elevator doors. They were pried open.
"What happened to the janitor?" I asked.

Flyes formed her hand into the shape of a pistol.
She pulled an invisible trigger.

48

"Whatever happened to Habir?" She asked.

I was clumsy with my next act, but I tried.

I wrapped an invisible cord around my neck. I pulled it up, to show that I was hanging.

"They put him on a leash?" Flyes asked.

"Something like that," I said. "We could have used leashes back then."

"For what?" She asked, looking at me.

"Dogs," I said.

***

So we walked further from Heaven, chains dragging at our ankles. They were weightless. We were weightless.

I wondered if anyone else felt weightless.

I was going to ask, but never did.

We passed by a man and a woman.

The woman had crazy, red hair and a huge purse.

She was holding hands with a well-groomed man in the best suit ever made. His hat had a brass plate. It said, "*Conductor,*" in etched letters.

I heard them talking.

The woman said something about a train. Something about *"Never again."* No one could see it, but her spine was broken in half.

The beautiful man agreed with her. He said something about fire. His whole body was a roasted skeleton.

***

Flyes and I kept going.

We could have walked forever. We never got tired or thirsty. I don't think anyone else got tired or thirsty.

I was going to ask, but never did.

We passed by two men and two women. The men were holding hands. So were the women.

All four of them walked together.

One man had ash all over his face.
The other had a pool cue in his anus.

One woman had no scalp.
The other had a hole in her forehead.

They were talking about how easy it was to be honest up here.

Apparently, back on Earth, they each had an affair with the person they were holding hands with. I heard them laughing about it, said they wished they had been more honest.

***

The most honest people I ever met were the dedicated believers of San Francisco, California. They really practiced what was preached to them. Most people from Earth had a hard time being honest, even to themselves.

I don't blame them.

I only followed my heart once. It led me onto a train. That train exploded.

The human heart was a big troublemaker.

But I do know some folks who followed their troublesome, human hearts, even to the end of time.

In fact, I saw those folks up here, while I walked with Flyes.

It was none other than the dedicated believers of San Francisco, California.

I had long since forgiven them for butchering my friends. I forgave them for what they did to so many nice people. And, God bless me, I even forgave them for killing my job at the Western Sun.

I felt relieved.

It was nice to forgive people.

It took me two-thousand years, but I did it.

***

Another thing about forgiveness:

It was easy when your perpetrator was hopeless.

That's how we found the disciples. Hopeless.

They were face-down in the clouds, embarrassed. They didn't want to look at anyone.

Flyes and I walked through that field of believers, stepping over bodies.

I tried to speak to some of them, but they refused to look at me. They really were ashamed.

It was ten-thousand human souls.

"Hey," I said, crouching next to one of them. "I forgive you."

It was a noble thing to say.

I was candid about it.

The believer shook his head. I think he was crying.

So we moved on.

The believers were still in their best Sunday clothes. Hindsight tells me one of them was sitting up, staring at the aether. He had a forty-five caliber revolver in his holster.

"Howdy," I said, forming my hand into a six-shooter.

"Howdy," he said back.

I looked at what he was projecting.

It was all black.

"What's that?" I asked.

"Everything," he said.

"Everything?" I asked.

He nodded. His eyes were wide open. He never blinked.

"Looks an awful lot like nothing," I said.

"It is," he said.

The clouds fizzled with static. I heard pops and grainy sand. His mind was an old, blank film, stuck on repeat.

I asked him if he could see anything in there.

He said he could not.

Apparently, his memories were dissolved by cocaine water. They were soup, swishing around in his imagination. His head was a bowl of diluted, meaningless thoughts.

All that was left were random sounds, things he might have heard before he died. They may have been from his childhood. They may have been from anywhere. They may not even have been true.

But there were sounds in that black void.

I closed my eyes and listened. I listened to the summary of this poor soul's life.

It was short and empty.

This was all it said:

Fire crackled. There was chanting and screaming. There was crying. I heard a saw blade rubbing through something hard and wet. I heard a river flowing. There were butterflies landing on the river. They landed everywhere. There were billions of them. I heard an explosion. I heard bricks collapse. I heard a truck crash into something hard. Glass shattered. I heard a driver door creak open. I heard someone fall out, splash into the street. I heard chains dragging over asphalt. I heard something deep in the distance, growing louder.

I think I heard someone saying please.

I didn't hear what they were asking for.

Somewhere, I heard a pistol click. It was loaded.

I heard the pop.

It was muffled by butterflies.

***

I looked at the disciple.

His eyes were dry and red. He never blinked. He stared at the clouds forever, as if he had no choice.

"What time is it?" He asked me, removing his pistol.

"Pardon?" I asked.

"I said, what time is it?"

I looked over at Flyes. She pointed her thumb backwards, telling me it was time to leave.

"No idea," I said. "No idea what time it is."

The disciple opened the pistol's chamber. There were invisible bullets in the cylinders.

"Feels like I've been going somewhere, been going for a long time," he said, closing the chamber. He clicked the hammer.

"But," the disciple said, "I never quite get there."

He slid the pistol into his mouth.

***

About all that:

Flyes and I left. We stood up, turned the other way, and walked as far as possible.

I paused, glancing back for a moment.

The disciple was still sitting there, pulling the trigger over and over again.

Nothing ever came out.

***

We were far from those poor, ten-thousand souls.

I used to be so angry at them.

Now, I realize they had no idea about anything.

They were fried on stimulants.

They might not even have hated us.

Up in God's front yard, I'm not even sure they were ashamed. They might have been totally braindead. When someone is braindead, they don't have much to do but lie down. Sometimes, they will try to shoot themselves in the mouth.

"I guess they were no different from anyone else," I said. "Terrified."

"I guess so," Flyes said.

People did all kinds of ridiculous things when they were afraid.

Some people were so afraid of Mother, they shot their loved ones to death.

Some people were so afraid of Hell, they killed everyone in San Francisco.

Some people were so afraid of God, they tried to kill Him too.

"Did you believe in God?" I asked Flyes. "Back home. Did you believe He was real?"

She shrugged.

"I guess so," she said. "Did you?"

"I guess so," I said. "Tried to forget about Him. Tried to imagine a life where He never existed. I was afraid of what would happen if we ever met."

"Well, I hope you're happy," Flyes said. "Now you might never meet."

I said that was fine.

She said she forgave me for being an idiot.

I said I forgave her for being a bitch.

We were holding hands.

We both forgave the disciples.

"I still remember that beach," I said. "Just barely, but I can see it."

Flyes agreed.

It was forming in the clouds.

49

I OPENED MY EYES for the last time on planet Earth.

I was dangling upside down over San Francisco, California. My four and a half inch penis was flapping in the wind.

We saw my road sign in the aether clouds.

It said, *"One Way,"* and it was planted in the gardens of Golgotha.

Yes, I was all the way up there, in the garden.

If I had sunk through the floor, I would have been in my father's old penthouse.

It was nice of the disciples to carry me to the roof.

It was nice of them to plant my road sign in the dirt, right on the edge. And they chained my ankle to the sign, dangled my naked body over the beach.

Hindsight tells me I was a symbol.

I was crucified up there. I was planted face to face with the death of humanity.

The disciples were proving that sin had been vanquished. They were telling the Creator that a terminus was no longer required: all malfeasance and monkey business had been dealt with.

***

Another thing about kindness:

The disciples propped me in front of a beautiful sunset. It was bleeding through the dark storm clouds. Aether tells me the sky was black and orange and purple.

I heard something deep. It bellowed in the horizon. It was getting closer.

I was hanging by my feet, of course. The universe was upside down. The ocean was the sky, and the sky was the ocean. Rain came from every direction. Beneath me was the beach. It was washing away with high tide.

Above me was God.
He was livid.

Right next to me was Flyes.

She was chained to a road sign, dangling from the edge. The disciples were kind enough to hang us together.

"Hey," I said, looking at her.

"Hey," Flyes said back. A line of blood trickled down her nose, over her forehead.

The city was burning.

I saw distant fire in the corner of my eye.

The whole place was dressed in lights for the end of the world.

"Beautiful," I said.

"What is?" She asked.

"Everything," I said, "even you."

I think Flyes was crying.

"Hey," I said, taking her hand. "At least you're not a raven any more."

I think Flyes smiled through her tears.

We were naked, bleeding, holding hands upside down in the apocalypse.

Something bellowed far away.

It was deep, as if the sky was opening up its mouth.

"Hopeman," Flyes said, squeezing my hand. It meant that she was afraid.

"I know," I said, squeezing her hand back.

***

I never thanked God for that afternoon.

Flyes was crying.

I saw our hands together.

I saw the waves crash onto the beach.

And I saw Mother.

I saw her upside down, growing larger in the horizon.

She was a wall of water, rolling through the sky.

She was getting closer.

The roaring was louder.

We closed our eyes.

I squeezed Flyes' hand.

It meant that we were naked, and bleeding, and that it was ok. It meant that we survived terrorism, and kidnapping, and explosions, and floods.

It meant that we masturbated too much and abused drugs.

It meant that we hated each other.

It meant that we loved each other.

It meant that we wasted our lives trying to find a way out. It meant that we found a way out, and it was inside us the whole time.

It meant that we were skinned alive by asphalt.
It meant that we still had our hearts.

It meant that we destroyed the world.
It meant that the world destroyed us.

It meant that we were just animals, looking for somewhere to sleep.

It meant that we were just babies, trying to grow up.
It meant that we grew up.
It meant that the universe grew up.
It meant that it got bigger and stranger every day.
It meant that we got bigger and stranger every day.

It meant that there was nothing else to mean.

It meant that I forgave everyone for everything.
It meant that they forgave me too.

It meant that we tried.

It meant that,
going two-million miles an hour through a dead universe,
we were happy.

50

The aether went black.

"That was it," I said, watching the clouds lose color, turning back into Heaven.
"That was it," Flyes said.

We had walked an awfully long way. The Pearly Gates were far in the distance.
"Well," I said. "I had no idea we could get this far."
There was no one else around.
We were still connected at the palms, our fingers locked.

***

Another thing about the clouds that day:
Jesus was there.

He was lying down by himself, about a mile from the Gates. His imagination was doing well. Aether clouds looked like an old, Middle Eastern village. I forgot Jesus had been a towel head.

"Mind if I sit here?" I asked.
"No problem at all," he said.

Flyes and I sat on either side of him.

I asked if God was outside the Gates. It was a big rumor going around.

"Nope," he said. "It's just me. Same face, same genes. We're always getting mixed up."

Another thing about Jesus: It's true about his beard. Looks just like the pictures back on Earth. He was also barefoot.

"Left the kicks at Papa's house," he said, pointing to his feet.

"Sorry," I said.

He waved lazily. It meant he could afford new shoes.

"What about you?" Jesus asked.

"Me?"

"Yeah, you lost your kicks."

"Oh," I said, looking at my own bare feet. "They're in a pile somewhere."

Jesus sympathized with that. He said lots of things were left in piles back on Earth.

"I didn't hate the Romans," he said, his imagination projecting a battlefield in the clouds. There was a pile of dead Roman soldiers. Blood was drooling down the pile, soaking into the sand.

"Poor kids," Jesus said. "Seventy-thousand in one day. Came straight to Papa." The aether focused on one face at the bottom of the pile. That face died with its eyes open. Jesus told me the guy had been stabbed through the abdomen five times.

"What a shame," I said.

"That's me," Jesus said.

"Really?" I asked.

"Really," he said.

I apologized on behalf of the Roman Empire.

Jesus waved his hand again. It meant that he could get a new body.

***

Jesus was projecting another memory.

It was a little girl sleeping on cold, hard soil. There was a shack around her. It was made of wooden planks, and no floor.

She had a star necklace and no shoes.

"Poor kid," Jesus said, pointing at the girl. A bayonet forced her up, out of the shack. It forced her into an assembly line.

She waited her turn to be strapped onto a conveyor belt. She was screaming.

That belt rolled slowly into a furnace.

"Me again," Jesus said. "All the Jews thought I had abandoned them. I didn't mean to."

I told him I believed him.

"I was a little girl," Jesus said. "I was a baby Jew. Jesus really did leave us, as far as I could tell. I hated him more than anyone."

***

I didn't mind watching Jesus' lives unfold.

I never asked for it, but he seemed interested.

His next time on Earth, Jesus was a cat.

He was resting on a sofa, sunlight blaring through the windows.

Then the windows exploded.

Some dogs jumped through.

The son of God was ripped to pieces.

"Looks rough," Flyes said.

Jesus nodded. He pointed to the first dog.

"That's you," he said.

"Me?" Flyes asked.

"You."

"Sorry," she said.

Jesus waved his hand lazily.

***

I asked Jesus why he was still in the first body he ever received.

He said he wasn't sure.

"Papa stopped sending me back after that last one," he said. "I kept getting killed, and I don't know why."

He said Papa felt sorry for him, kept him in Heaven for a while.

"And," Jesus said, "that's when the monkey business started."

***

He told me about Heaven.

"The other side is great," he said. "I have no idea what it looks like any more, but it was great, I can tell you that."

"No idea what it looks like?" I asked.

"Nope," he said. Apparently, if you went to Heaven, you forgot what the outside looked like. And if you left, you forgot what the inside looked like.

"But it was great," Jesus said. "People didn't have to wait around like they do now. I even had my own place."

"Really?" I asked, interested in what type of life Jesus had. I wanted to tell him all about my old plans. He would have loved my small farm, my vegetables. God might overhear us, and be impressed that I would share my produce.

"Parties every night," Jesus said. "Bottles of milk and honey. Never really had a childhood back on Earth. I kept dying. So, it was time to live a little, get it out of my system."

"Oh," I said.

"It was wild in there," Jesus said. "One time, Michael broke the chandelier. He jumped on, and said, *'who needs wings when you've got balls!'*"

I asked for an invitation.

Apparently, that wouldn't happen for a while.

"Papa and I had some words about that," Jesus said. "He told me no more parties, I was trashing the place. So I got pissed, and left. I kicked the mailbox on my way out. Papa saw it. Yelled at me to '*clean that shit up.*'"

I asked if he cleaned up that shit.

He said he did.

Imagine that: the son of God bent over drunk, picking up all the letters he had kicked from the mailbox.

"Reminds me," he said, pulling a roll of parchment from his pocket. "This here's for you."

"Really?" I asked.

"Really," he said. "From someone named Roselle. She came to the parties, I think. Got kicked out with everyone else."

"Kicked out?"

"Yeah. After I left, Papa told everyone to get out."

"Where did she go?" I asked.

Jesus shrugged.

"No idea," he said. "Big place out here."

51

I HELD THE PARCHMENT in my fingers.
It was paper from Heaven. It was ink from an angel.

"Thank you," I said to the son of God.
"No problem," Jesus said. He was watching the Middle Eastern village again, pointing to a wooden chair. It was in some workshop.
"See that chair?" He said.
I did see it. It was beautiful.
"I made that," Jesus said.
"It's beautiful," I replied.
He nodded, said he wished he could have sat in it before he died. Jesus told me how the chair somehow ended up in Pilate's living room.
"Interesting," I said.
He nodded.

Jesus and Flyes went on talking about something. She couldn't believe she had been a dog. She couldn't believe how long her soul had been around.
And they went on, talking about Earth.

It was background noise to me.
I unrolled the parchment.
This is what it said:

"Dear Hope,

It's Rose Petal.

By the time you read this, God will be opening the Gates.
How do I know?
I'm in Heaven now. I know lots of things.
But I won't be here for long.

For some reason, I never got sent back to Earth after getting shot.
I think God felt bad for me, thought I would keep getting in trouble.
He was probably right.
My other lives were full of trouble.

Apparently, I am five-thousand years old.
That's what Jesus tells me. He knows an awful lot about who we
were, what we did.
On my first try, I remember sitting in my bathtub in Jerusalem.
I can still see the sunset. It was purple and orange. I was beautiful
back then, my naked skin dripping with warm, soapy water.
And I remember being married to a brave soldier. He was
handsome, and deeply in love with me. He loved everyone.
But, somehow I ended up having sex with the King of Israel.
Somehow, my husband died.

I was born so many times, Hopeman.
For the most part, I have no idea what happened in those five-
thousand years. They might as well not have happened. Part of me wishes
they never did. But then I would never have met you. You were the only
real friend I ever had.

Oh, here is one more thing I remember about Earth.
I know what I was before my short life as Roselle:
I was in love with two women.
One of them was my wife. The other was a receptionist at a
roadside motel in Reno, Nevada. She knew I was married. She didn't
care. I drove an eighteen-wheeler back then. I always chose the shifts that
went through Reno. And if I didn't get them, I made my routes take a

scenic detour. That scene was always the same: a dusty motel with cable television and a spring mattress. The mattress squeaked every time I passed through Reno.

Somehow, my wife found out about all the squeaking.
She flushed her wedding ring down the toilet.
She got into a car and drove east. Never saw her again.
The receptionist left too. She left after I became 'pathetic.'
That was her word for it. Pathetic.
Apparently, that's what a river of whiskey did to a man.
Made him pathetic.
Gave him liver cancer.
Gave him silence.
Gave him the chance to drive his truck off the Golden Gate Bridge, into the ocean, at nine in the morning.

And then, I was Roselle.
And then, you were Hopeman.
And then, we were together for five years.
I have no idea what we had in common back then.
I have no idea how we got along so well.
Maybe it was because we really were the same age, and still are.
What difference does it make, when our souls live forever?

Also, as I write this letter, you are officially twenty-nine. Congratulations.
And congratulations to me for remembering your birthday.

This scroll is supposed to come to you in a dream, or however the angels do it. They are mysterious about that.

By the way, I hear Jesus and God arguing. Something about no more parties, something about being a mess. So, I think Jesus might leave soon.
I am leaving too.
I write this before I get kicked out. Everyone is getting kicked out.
We trashed the place.

When Jesus got home, there was a huge party. It went on for years with no end in sight. I think Michael wasn't getting enough attention, so he jumped on the chandelier.

And so on.

So, how do I know God will be opening the Gates for you?
Well, I don't.
All I know is this:

He lost the keys to the front door.

It's true.
Jesus had them in the front pocket of his robe. When the chandelier crashed into the bar, Jesus got splattered with milk and honey.
So, he changed into another robe right before God busted the party.
And so on.

God won't listen to any of us, so there's no warning Him about those keys.
I guess He'll be looking all over, trying to find them.
And I suspect He will find them.
He might say He's locking you out, but I think He's just embarrassed about the whole thing. So when you get inside, don't mention it.
And don't mention planet Earth. He really was pissed at us for trashing it. And then we made a huge mess in His kingdom. God is sensitive about keeping things neat, so just listen to Him. It's Heaven. It's not that hard to get along.

For your sake, I hope everything works out.
It no longer bothers me.

By the time you read this, I will have wandered into infinity.
It's strange out there, on the other side of the Gates.
I like that.

There is some kind of energy or gravity phenomenon. I don't know much about it.

All I know is that, unless you walk straight out of the Gates, you will circle back around to where you started. It's true. Some kind of energy, or magnetism.

But, if you walk straight out of the Gates, it won't happen like that.

Somehow, if you stay perfectly straight and keep walking, you're free. Eventually, that magnetism will disappear. Nothing to pull you back. Lost at sea with no lifeboat.

What's out there? I have no idea.
There might be nothing.
It might never end.
There might not even be a way back.

But I'm going.
I'm going, and I don't know why.
I guess I like the strange.
I've never been good at staying in one place, not in five-thousand years.
Maybe it's God's way of telling me to figure out what's over there. He's mysterious about that, about communicating.

Anyway, I'm fine up here, thanks for asking. I was scared at first, scared of being lost forever. But now, even before I leave the Gates and forget this place forever, I am happy. I always knew there was something like courage in me. A shame it took five-thousand years to find it. But now, I'm addicted to finding new things. So here goes Roselle, strolling through clouds on two, bare feet.

It might be my last adventure, so I want to tell you this:
No matter what's over there, you'll always be the first friend I ever had.

We met when you were five. I died when you were ten.
You still had fat from your baby years. You cried and had no friends your own age.

I was at my worst.
I was eighteen.

I slept with your father.

*You and I were a mess. We were horrible, gross,
and pretty cool.*

*So, have fun in there.
Don't litter, and don't lose your keys.*

I love you, Hopeman.

52

ANOTHER THING about Heaven:
The Gates opened up.

Roselle was right. God must have found the keys.
Maybe the angels finished cleaning up Earth, and they returned to clean up Heaven.
Maybe Michael was sweeping broken glass and found Jesus' robe.
And so on.

I still remember when the Gates opened.
I was sitting on the clouds. In front of me were two people: a naked, bleeding woman, and the son of God. They were standing, looking at something in the distance. And they spoke to me, something about a crowd forming, something about the Gates.
I was deaf. I was reading the final words on a sheet of old parchment. I might have read them over and over, trying to tattoo the letters onto my brain.

Another thing about that moment:
I didn't realize how long I had been sitting there.
I was trapped in a daydream.
My mind fell through the clouds, backwards in time, and landed in my bed. It was easy. I sank right though. I imagined a

rainy, Saturday morning in Oakland, California. There were butterflies landing on the roof, and Roselle making breakfast downstairs. And when I went down into the kitchen, she had a full, smiling mouth.

"Hey," Jesus said, snapping his fingers.
I looked up.
He was pointing towards Heaven.

There was a crowd surrounding God's front door.
It was open.

***

We stared at it for a long time.
Jesus looked surprised, said that Papa must have finally found the house keys. He explained how he left them in his robe. Told me how that poor robe hadn't been washed in years.

So, the Gates really opened.
White mist shrouded everything inside.
I saw a crowd of souls melting through that mist. They shuffled closer, disappearing,
It was billions of them.
It was beautiful.

Another thing about that mist:
Bulgruf melted through.

That's what Jesus told me.
"I know the big guy was on your mind," he said. "Wanted to let you know he's ok."

Jesus was right. There was no arguing with the son of God. I was wondering if my old, fat friend made it to Heaven. I wondered if he had anyone to walk with.
"He's holding hands," Jesus said to me.
"Really?" I asked. "With who?"

Jesus shrugged.
"You wouldn't recognize her. Has a tattoo, I think."

***

Jesus told me all about the people he could see in that crowd.
His vision was great. It went for miles.

Apparently, everyone was smiling.
They had no idea how they did it, but someone must have apologized correctly.
Humans, God bless them, thought they did something right. They deserved to smile. It was nice to get along with the creator of the universe.

Also, my parents were there. They were holding hands, walking through the mist. Jesus said they were on good terms with God, despite the holes in their heads.

***

Jesus said something about another naked man. He was old, white, donning underwear and a bath towel. His fingers were in the calloused palms of an old farmer.
Apparently, that farmer was shaking his head playfully.
It meant he didn't give a damn where he was.

The naked man gave him a playful tug.
It meant to stop being so difficult.

***

There were two towel heads holding hands.
A man and a woman, neither of them wearing towels.
The man had barbed wire around his neck.
The woman looked fine. She was old and beautiful.

***

Jesus looked back at us.
"Well," he said. "You guys ready?"

I thought about that for a moment, if I was ready. I thought about forgetting everything out here. Inside Heaven, I could write my stories on heavenly parchment. There would be golden streets, and a little house on the shore. I could live there, and wade through the ocean every day. The ocean would be clean, and have gentle waves. It would never want to hurt a human soul.

I thought about all that.

Then, I stood up, brushed the invisible dirt off my clothes.

I put a hand on Jesus' shoulder, and said,
"Thanks again, for the letter."

"Hey, no problem," he said, taking my other hand. "Thank me later, after you spend a night in my guest house. You're going to love it."

I told him not to worry about that.
I was leaving.

***

It's true.
I died and never went to Heaven.
I stood about a mile from the open Gates, face to face with the son of God.
Then, I turned the other way, and left.

He asked me why.
I told him it was a Sunday. I had a letter to send.

***

Another thing about my memory:

There is almost nothing left.

So far, everything I have told you is on the backs of envelopes and scrolls. Jesus gave them to me before I left. Apparently, they flew out when he kicked the mailbox. He'd been carrying them around for years.

And Jesus gave me a quill and ink.

He said that ink was great, it never ran out. It's what God himself used to write letters.

I thanked him again, told him I always wanted to be a writer.

My memory of Flyes is gone.

I have no idea what her face looks like.

I have no idea what her hands feel like.

She looked at me before I left.

She said something that I can't remember. Something about strawberries, and a farm. Something about trees.

And we hugged one more time.

I told her something too. Something about a train, or maybe a truck. Something about a cliff, or a road sign.

Then I was gone.

***

So, I have been walking closer and closer to infinity.

Along the way, I scribbled everything that came to me. My life, my friends' lives. The truths, the myths. All of it. I can't tell the difference anymore. But I know this: I used that magical ink to write all my memories onto the backs of envelopes.

And then I put each envelope on the clouds.

There's no wind up here, thank God.

Maybe, when everyone gets sent back to Earth and destroys it again, they will return to God's front yard. Maybe they will see my trail of letters. Maybe they will finally read all the clever things I wanted to say on Earth, but never did.

Maybe they will follow my stories all the way into infinity.

Maybe they will find me at the end.

Maybe they will find Roselle.

We will both be naked, covered in blood.

We won't have any memory.

I will have forgotten who I am, and where I was going.

She will have forgotten who she is, and where she came from.

Maybe there will be a garden there, with just enough vegetables. And there might trees for miles, with a little patch of strawberries.

And it might rain just enough.

Or there might be nothing at all.

I might walk naked forever, dragging a chain around my foot.

***

So here is my final envelope.

It will be on the clouds, waiting for anyone foolish enough to come this far.

If they do find it, God bless.

If they don't, God bless.

I want to lose my mind knowing that I had been honest. My last memory is about to drip away from me. It tells me that we all had a hard time being honest.

***

So, here goes the drip.
Here goes my honesty.
This is all that remains of Hopeman, or whoever I am:

"Dear God,
Dear Bulgruf and Flyes and Henry,
Dear Arthur and disciples,
Dear Mom and Dad,
Dear Javeer Assmoo,
Dear Roselle,
Dear Mother,

Hold my hand when the world ends."

Frank Donato is a writer and painter from Baltimore, Maryland. He wrote all this in the basement of his parents' home, instead of studying. Fortunately for everyone, he is moving to Cape Charles, Virginia, as a kayak tour guide.

This is his first novel.

Made in the USA
Middletown, DE
31 May 2016